"It's the best date I've ever been on,"

Reese assured Sophie, his niece. "And are you having fun?" Reese turned to his other "date" for the evening.

"I always have fun here," Emily said. "The Goodtime Café is the best place in town for a date. All the high school kids come here."

"And then they fall in love," the child said. "And then they get married and have babies."

"Yeah, I guess that's how it happens," Emily agreed, but averted her eyes from Sophie's very attractive uncle who was sitting across from her.

Reese smiled and Emily's heart skipped a beat. "I guess you could say the café has a reputation for bringing people together," he said, silently challenging her to meet his gaze.

He was flirting with her. Suddenly the music stopped and the room grew quiet....

Dear Reader,

Four special women shatter the barricades they've built around their dreams, in Silhouette Romance this month. Be it openly defying the life role set out for them or realizing their life's ambition, these independent ladies represent the type of aspirational heroines we're looking for in Silhouette Romance.

Myrna Mackenzie launches our newest trilogy, SHAKESPEARE IN LOVE, with *Much Ado About Matchmaking* (SR #1786) in which a woman who doesn't think she's special or beautiful enough for the worldly hero finally gets the courage to listen to her heart. *The Texan's Suite Romance* (SR #1787) rounds out Judy Christenberry's LONE STAR BRIDES continuity and features a woman who knows Mr. Right when she meets him but now must help him heal enough to let love back into his lonely life. When her screenplay is made into a movie set on her family's ranch, one woman thinks she's fulfilled all her dreams…until she meets one very handsome stuntman. Watch this drama unfold in *Lights, Action…Family!* (SR #1788)—the concluding romance in Patricia Thayer's LOVE AT THE GOODTIME CAFÉ miniseries. Finally, Crystal Green wraps up the BLOSSOM COUNTY FAIR series with *Her Gypsy Prince* (SR #1789) in which a sheltered woman bucks her family's wishes to pursue a forbidden love.

And be sure to come back next month when Elizabeth Harbison puts a modern spin on Shakespeare's *Taming of the Shrew.*

Happy reading,

Ann Leslie Tuttle
Associate Senior Editor

Please address questions and book requests to:
Silhouette Reader Service
U.S.: 3010 Walden Ave., P.O. Box 1325, Buffalo, NY 14269
Canadian: P.O. Box 609, Fort Erie, Ont. L2A 5X3

PATRICIA THAYER

Lights, Action... Family!

Love at the
Goodtime Café

SILHOUETTE *Romance*®

Published by Silhouette Books

America's Publisher of Contemporary Romance

SILHOUETTE BOOKS

ISBN 0-373-19788-8

LIGHTS, ACTION...FAMILY!

Copyright © 2005 by Patricia Wright

This edition published by arrangement with Harlequin Books S.A.

Visit Silhouette Books at www.eHarlequin.com

Printed in U.S.A.

Books by Patricia Thayer

PATRICIA THAYER

has been writing for sixteen years and has published over twenty books with Silhouette. Her books have been nominated for the National Readers' Choice Award, Virginia Romance Writers of America's Holt Medallion, Orange Rose Contest and a prestigious RITA® Award. In 1997, *Nothing Short of a Miracle* won the *Romantic Times* Reviewers' Choice Award for Best Special Edition.

Thanks to the understanding men in her life—her husband of thirty-plus years, Steve, and her three grown sons and two grandsons—Pat has been able to fulfill her dream of writing romance. Another dream is to own a cabin in Colorado, where she can spend her days writing and her evenings with her favorite hero, Steve. She loves to hear from readers. You can write to her at P.O. Box 6251, Anaheim, CA 92816-0251, or check her Web site at www.patriciathayer.com for upcoming books.

To Daralynn.

You are a wonderful wife to my son, and mother to my grandsons, Harrison and Connor. Even when things get tough, you take them in stride with your unwavering strength and determination...and always with love.

Chapter One

The Arizona territory, June 6, 1904
Today, my beautiful bride, Rebecca, and I found
the perfect home site, a lush valley surrounded by
majestic mountains. This is where it will all be-
gin....
Jacob's Journal

From the top of his jet-black Stetson, to his oversize
belt buckle, right down to his scuffed Tony Lama boots,
he was all cowboy.

Emily Hunter should know because she'd been
around them all her life, the real and the phony. And,
oh yes, he was definitely of the real variety.

She leaned against the café counter and boldly eyed
the man who filled the doorway. He had broad shoul-

ders covered by a sand-colored Western shirt, washed-out jeans encased his narrow hips and long muscular legs. She raised her gaze to his chiseled face and deep-set eyes, and hoped he would come closer so she could see their color.

The stranger gave her a quick nod in greeting and suddenly her heartbeat sped up. Before she could recip-rocate, he turned away as a little girl appeared at his side. She had a tousled mass of brunette ringlets that cir-cled her round face. Her eyes mirrored her father's in-cluding the long black lashes.

The man took his daughter's hand as they made their way to the counter. He effortlessly lifted the tiny girl on-to a seat. She seemed to be about four years old and was as cute as could be. Of course, just look at her father. And look she did as he pulled off his hat, revealing thick, nearly black hair and dark-as-midnight eyes. He straddled the stool and rested his large forearms on the counter.

Emily quickly halted the direction of her thoughts. The man was married with a child, for heaven's sake. She went off to fill two water glasses, reminding her-self she was here to work. After she graduated college she'd thought her days as a waitress were over. Then a good family friend, Sam Price, owner of the fifties-style diner, Good Time Café, needed someone to fill in when his regular waitress called in sick. She had a few days to kill until things were set up at the Double H, so why not?

With her best smile, Emily set the water in front of

her customers. "Good morning," she said as she handed the man a breakfast menu. "What can I get for you?" She met the stranger's dark gaze and found breathing difficult.

Darn if he didn't look even better close up.

"I'll have coffee to start."

She turned and took the pot off the warmer. After she placed a mug of the hot brew in front of the man, she looked at the child. She was wearing a faded pink cotton T-shirt that was wrinkled and too big. So her dad wasn't a fashion expert. "And what will you have to drink, milk or juice?" she asked the little girl.

"Bring her milk," the man said, then glanced at the child. "Sophie, what do you want to eat?"

The tiny girl looked up with dark eyes that seemed too large for her face, then silently shrugged her shoulders. Emily decided the shy youngster needed a little coaxing.

"Sophie. That's a pretty name," she began. "I'm Emily. It sure is nice to meet you. You must be what…about four years old?" The girl nodded. "You know when I was about your age my daddy used to bring me here. My favorite thing was Sam's blueberry pancakes." She leaned closer to the child and whispered. "You want to try some?"

When there wasn't any answer, the stranger said, "My niece is a little shy with strangers."

Reece McKellen didn't expect Sophie to answer the waitress. She hadn't said more than a few dozen words to him since she'd come to live with him nearly a month ago. Not that he blamed her. She'd been through far too much for a child. If it were possible he wanted to erase all the bad from her short life. Right now, it was going to be a full time job trying to reassure the child that he wouldn't abandon her like everyone else in her short life.

"You can bring us both the blueberry pancakes and two glasses of milk."

"Good choice," the waitress said and tossed him another smile.

Reece watched the pretty brunette walk off and felt a stir of awareness. She had large blue eyes and a full wide mouth that would tempt any man. Her fitted uniform outlined a shapely body and her long trim legs got his blood pumping. He shifted on his stool. A month ago he wouldn't hesitate to give someone like Emily his full attention, but his once solitary life had changed drastically in a matter of weeks.

Now, he had the responsibility of his niece. Somehow he had to figure out how to take care of a child and fulfill his commitment on this new job.

Already the social worker assigned to his niece's case wasn't happy that he had taken Sophie out of state and on location for the next few months. But what else could he do? He needed to make a living, and more importantly, he needed to make a permanent home for Sophie. And that was the reason he came to Haven, Arizona.

Reece took a sip of coffee, and looked down at Sophie. She was a miniature version of Carrie when she was that age. A slow ache settled in his chest. Although he might not be the best choice for a father, he wasn't going to renege on a promise again.

Emily felt the man's formidable presence all the way from the end of the counter. She tried to ignore it, but no such luck. She picked up their orders from the pass-through window and carried the food to the counter.

"Here we are, two blueberry pancake specials," she said, surprised to find she was eager to see the little girl's reaction. She set the first plate down in front of the man then turned to Sophie.

"Sam does a treat when special girls come in." She set down the stack of pancakes topped with a whipped cream smiley face decorating the top.

"See, Sam drew you a picture." She enjoyed the child's surprised look. Emily glanced at the uncle. "I hope you don't mind the whipped cream."

He gave her a half smile. "Not at all. As you can see, Sophie here could stand a few extra calories."

Emily had many questions about her new customers, but they were none of her business. The two were just passing through town. "Where are you headed?" she asked, assuring herself she was just making conversation.

The man poured maple syrup over his pancakes. "Right here."

"You're moving to Haven?"

"Temporarily." He dug into his stack and took a bite. "I'm working outside of town for the next few months."

Okay, now the man peaked her curiosity. Besides, living in a small town, it was hard to stay out of everyone's business. Maybe he was going to work for one of the ranches in the area, though it would be unusual for anyone to be hiring extra hands during the summer. She wondered if his work would be nearby and if she would be running into him often. Well, it really didn't matter where he would be working or how good-looking he was. She had other things on her plate right now.

Her career had to take first priority in her life.

"Well, good luck," she said and walked away. Emily grabbed a rag and began polishing the other end of the empty counter.

The Good Time Café, with its good food and friendly atmosphere, was a popular hangout in town, and had been for years. But at ten o'clock on a weekday morning the place was deserted. The cowboy and the cute little girl were the only diners at the moment.

Actually after the busy shift, Emily was glad for he reprieve. In truth, she'd been distracted all morning. She couldn't wait to get back to the ranch and see what was going on. Had her brother finished building the replica homestead? Had the film crew arrived? Every day for the past two weeks, something new and exciting had been going on. When Sam asked her to fill in at the café, she hesitated, but decided she needed to get away from the project. She also knew that her brothers, Nate and Shane, weren't unhappy to see her go. They both wanted her out of their hair.

So she'd been a little excited about the project. It

wasn't every day that she got her screenplay, *Hunter's Haven,* made into a movie. And it was being filmed right where the original story took place, at the Double H Ranch. Excitement surged through her as she made her way over to the jukebox. She reached into her pocket for some quarters. After inserting them into the machine, she selected some of her favorites from Sam's oldies-but-goodies songs, and the silent room was soon filled with the voices of The Temptations singing "My Girl."

Emily began to sway to the easy rhythm as she danced though the tables to the red vinyl booths that lined the windows. Outside, she noticed the dusty, crew cab truck with a trailer parked in the lot across Maple Street. She noticed the plates weren't Arizona, but couldn't make out the name of the state.

The music ended and was replaced by another song, a blues ballad by Percy Sledge, "When a Man Loves a Woman." Emily moved to the music as she cleaned, then turned and caught the cowboy's reflection in the mirror over the counter. He took a long sip of coffee as his attention settled on her.

Emily froze as her eyes locked with the stranger's. The sultry singer's voice seemed to create an intimacy between them, and neither seemed to want to the connection to end. But then Sam suddenly called her name.

Embarrassed, she jerked her gaze away and went to the kitchen window angry with herself for letting the cowboy get to her. The man was only going to be around temporarily. And she had to stay focused on her movie.

After answering Sam's question, she returned to her tasks and found little Sophie watching her. Emily couldn't help but be drawn to the child's solemn expression. They exchanged looks as she continued her work, keeping time with the rhythm of the jukebox tunes. Finally the child gave a half smile, which disappeared as quickly as it had appeared.

Emily walked behind the counter. "Well, how was your breakfast?"

"Great," the cowboy told her as he pulled bills from his wallet. "We better get going." Just then the girl tugged on her uncle's sleeve causing him to lean down to her level.

The man glanced up at Emily. "Ah, where's your rest room?"

"In back," she said. "If you want, I'll take her."

The man looked doubtful. "Sophie, will you let Emily take you?"

The girl's eyes widened, then she nodded.

"Okay, Sophie, come with me." Emily held out her hand and together they walked down the hall. After the child finished, Emily made sure she washed her hands and face, and decided to do a little more grooming. She went to retrieve her purse from the cabinet in back.

"How about if I brush your hair?" When the child didn't object, Emily put her in front of the mirror and gently drew the brush through the tangled ringlets. "You have such pretty curls."

Once the child was freshened up, they returned hand in hand to the front of the cafe where the uncle was waiting. "Thank you," he said as Sophie took his hand.

"No problem. We girls have to take care of each other," Emily said, realizing she didn't want them leave.

"I guess we should go now." He reached for his hat. "Thanks for your help… Emily."

"My pleasure," she said, meaning it. "Maybe I'll see you around town." Whoa, where did that come from?

"I doubt it. I'm going to be pretty busy. You could help me with some directions, though."

"Sure, where are you headed?"

"The Double H Ranch."

Emily tried not to react. Was Nate hiring? "I doubt they're hiring right now."

"I'll take my chances. Do you know the way?"

"Just head back out to the highway and go east about ten miles until you reach Hunter Ridge Road. Turn left and go another mile and you'll run right into it."

He nodded. With a tug on the child's hand, they walked out the door. Sophie looked over her shoulder and waved shyly with her free hand.

Something tightened around Emily's heart. Through the window her gaze followed them as the man helped his niece into the truck. Both the truck and trailer looked like they'd covered a lot of miles. Was that where they lived while traveling from job to job? Where was the child's mother and father?

"Sam!" she called, pulling off her apron. "I need to get back to the ranch. Can you handle things on your own?"

The husky man in his late fifties stepped out from the kitchen. He scratched his head. "Emily, I really could use your help during the lunch shift."

"Margaret can handle it," she said.

"Sure but, Em, you know Shane and Nate can handle things...."

"I know that. I'm not going back to bug them, I've got to talk to Nate about giving a man a job."

After a stop at the store for some groceries, snacks and drinks, and to gas up the truck, Reece headed out of town toward the Double H. This new job wasn't going to be easy to pull off. Not with a child in tow. The stunts were pretty basic, just some trick riding. But Reece had a child depending on him now and his commitment to Sophie changed everything. He'd signed on for the stunt job before he even knew of his niece's existence. The producer, Jason Michael, had just about begged Reece to work on this movie. If the producer hadn't been so persistent, he'd never have agreed to take the job. Jason had assured Reece that they'd work out housing and childcare once he arrived on location.

Reece's grip tightened on the steering wheel. He wished he had a permanent home for Sophie now. Hopefully after this last job, he could head to Texas and buy that small ranch he'd always wanted. And he could make a home for Sophie.

Suddenly years of guilt washed over him as distant memories came flooding back. His sister, Carrie, had been three years his junior. He wasn't sure if they even had the same father. However, if they'd had the choice, neither one of them would have claimed Gina McKellen for their mother. No matter how bad it got, Carrie and Reece had had each other. When their mother took off, child services stepped in and they'd been separated. Reece had promised he'd find Carrie wherever she wound up and that they would be together again.

He'd been out of foster care a while before he finally located her. Bitter and street tough, Carrie had hooked up with a bad crowd, and hadn't wanted his help…until her death. And then he'd been shocked when he'd learned that his sister wanted him to raise her only child.

So at thirty-two Reece had suddenly become a parent. He hadn't thought twice about taking Sophie. She was his family. And he hadn't realized how much that mattered to him until he'd gotten to social services in Dallas and saw this tiny, lost-looking kid. She looked up at him with those big brown eyes and said, "Unca Reece" and his fate was sealed. At that moment Reece vowed that he'd give her the home he was never able to give Carrie.

He might not be the best father material. God knew he hadn't had much experience in that department, but Sophie's chances were better with him than in foster care. Now, he just had to make a permanent home for his new charge. His one bedroom apartment in L.A. was only passable for the social worker. Owning his own ranch had been his plan for years, and the reason he'd gotten into stunt work.

He had an eye on a small place in West Texas where he could breed horses and maybe run a few head of cattle. Although he'd saved about everything he could, he still hadn't accumulated the amount he needed. So this job for Jason Michael's Production should about get him the rest of the money, and convince the caseworker, Mrs. Reynolds, that he was serious about making a home for Sophie. But for now, since he didn't have permanent custody of his niece, he'd had to get permission to bring Sophie to the movie location. He also had to report in, and might even be visited by the local child services authorities.

Reece blew out a long breath. Job number one was to find suitable housing for Sophie and himself while they were in Haven. Then he had to find someone to take care of Sophie while he worked on the movie set. His thoughts turned to the waitress. She would be good with his niece, but he doubted she would give up a permanent job to baby-sit. And with the sparks that had flashed between them back at the café, she would be one complication too many. He already had enough to deal with with Sophie and the new job.

He just hoped Jason had those details all worked out.

Seeing the sign, Reece turned onto the road that led to the Double H Ranch. He gazed out the window at the view. The rust and brown hues of the mountain range stood out against a rich blue sky. It was breathtaking. Although he was a Texas boy, it wouldn't be a hardship enjoying this beautiful country for the next few months.

Reece drove under the archway that announced the ranch's proprietor Nate Hunter. Envy ate at him as rows of white fencing, surrounding a bright-red barn along with several white outbuildings appeared. To his left a horse trotted around a large corral, reminding him that his own mounts, Toby and Shadow, needed attention.

A yellow, two-story house trimmed in white came into view. There was a circular driveway lined with multicolored flowers that led to a huge wraparound porch adorned with a wooden swing and several wicker chairs. The whole scene was an invitation to just sit and relax.

"Look at the big house," Sophie gasped from the back seat.

"It sure is big," he answered, enjoying her rare stab at conversation.

"And pretty flowers," she whispered.

Reece smiled as he headed the truck toward where a posted sign directed the film crew to the back side of the barn. There were a few cars there, but not any crew. Great. He had two horses that had been confined in a trailer longer than they should be. He parked under a large tree, shading the truck from the hot August sun and turned to Sophie.

"Hey, sweetie, I need to get Shadow and Toby out of the trailer. So you stay here. I'll leave the air on so you should stay cool enough. Okay?"

She nodded. "'Kay," she answered and grabbed the raggedy bear off the seat and hugged it. Since the day he'd met his niece, she'd been inseparable from her stuffed friend. It had been the only toy the child had with her. And although Reece had taken her to a toy store, she hadn't found anything she wanted to replace the bear. By some miracle he'd managed to get her to leave it in the truck while they went into the café.

He climbed out, walked to the back of the trailer and lowered the gate. Usually on a movie location, he just bunked in the truck cab, but he couldn't do that with Sophie. Movie companies often supplied housing on location, but such accommodations were reserved for the headlining actors. Stunt people never received such preferential treatment. He had no idea what kind of arrangements Jason had made for him. He just hoped it was close to the ranch, and a suitable sitter for Sophie.

He walked up the ramp to the horses he had trained to do the stunt work. "How are you guys doing?" he spoke in a soothing voice as he ran a hand over Toby's rump. A high pitched whinny told Reece that both animals wanted out. Now. He unfastened Toby's reins, then gently nudged the horse to back up. It took some time, but he got the horse down the ramp. Toby immediately began to dance around in the grass, letting Reece know he wanted to run.

"Sorry, fella, there isn't time right now." He led the horse to the corral fence and tied him there and went back to the trailer.

He was bringing a black mare, Shadow, down the ramp when he heard a female voice say, "I see you found your way."

Reece swung around to find the brunette waitress standing beside the trailer. This time she was dressed in jeans, boots and a blue blouse that matched her eyes.

Damn, if she didn't look even better than she had in her uniform.

"Yeah, thanks for the directions." He led Shadow to the corral railing and tied him securely. He glanced over his shoulder to discover the woman was following him. "Look, if I led you to think you and I could…get together…I'm sorry. Like I said I'm going to be real busy—"

Her back straightened. "You think I followed you because I want to start up something with you?"

"Look…it's not that I'm not interested, it's just that I've got my hands full right now."

Emily was fuming. If he hadn't been tending to his horses she would have hauled off and smacked him.

"Pretty sure of yourself, cowboy," she said from between clenched teeth. To think she rushed out here to put in a good word for him with Nate. Of course she'd told herself it was strictly for the child. "I only came out here to help you."

"Well, I thank you, but I can handle things from here." He went back to the truck leaving Emily with her mouth open.

She went marching after him. "I doubt it. Not if you came here looking for work. Nate is—"

"Hey, Em," the familiar voice of her brother called to her. "I knew you couldn't stay away."

Nate Hunter was dressed in his khaki sheriff's uniform. His tenure as the town's lawman was soon to be a thing of the past. His retirement was only a few months away. He would be hanging up his sheriff's hat about the same time his son was to be born. Then he could be a full-time rancher, wood carver and most important to Nate, a husband and father.

"Someone has to keep an eye on you guys," she told him, still miffed that everyone wanted her out of the way while they finished the movie set.

Her big brother's attention turned to the new arrival. "Hi, I'm Nate Hunter." He held out his hand.

The man shook it. "Reece McKellen."

Nate smiled. "We've been expecting you."

Emily was totally confused. "You've hired him?"

Nate gave her a strange look. "No, sis, Jason did. Remember? The movie's producer?"

Emily could feel the heat rise to her cheeks. "I didn't realize." She sent him an accusing glance. "You could have said something."

If it were any consolation Reece looked just as confused as she did.

"Em, meet Reece," Nate continued. "He's the wrangler and stuntman on the movie. Reece, this is Emily Hunter, the author of *Hunter's Haven*."

Reece sure didn't see this one coming. He quickly recovered and tipped his hat, murmuring, "Ma'am." Then he turned headed back to the truck. So the Good Time Café waitress was also the screenwriter and author Emily Hunter. Just Great. Not that he had any hangups working with a woman, but there was no denying that there were sparks between them and that could mean trouble. If he let it. He shook away the thought. No way. He had to concentrate on just two things, this stunt job and his new role as Sophie's parent.

He opened the truck door and realized that even with the air going it was still warm inside. So was his niece.

"I'm sorry, sweetheart." He unbuckled her seat belt and lifted her out of her seat in the truck and onto the grass. Then reached in the cooler he always kept in the cab and took out a bottle of water. After he made sure that Sophie drank enough, he took some himself.

He'd always liked movie work, and he was good at his job. The one positive thing about his time in foster care was he'd been sent to live on a ranch. He'd taken to horses immediately and as long as he'd gotten his chores done, he'd been allowed to ride. As he gotten older, he'd become somewhat of an expert rider, and one of the best around to do horse stunts.

According to the director of this movie, Trent Justice, this movie's stunts would be a piece of cake. Just some fast riding scenes and saving the leading lady, Jennifer Tate, from a runaway horse.

Not for the first time Reece wondered if this particular job was more trouble than it was worth. Maybe it would be too much of a hassle to work while Sophie was still adjusting to her mother's death. Would it be better if he cut his losses and headed to Texas? He could get a job as a ranch manager. Though it wouldn't pay as well as stunt work, he could put a stable roof over Sophie's head.

And there would be no Emily Hunter to distract him. She was the kind of woman who could cause him to lose his focus. She might even make him think about completing his family. Not that his track record had been good when it came to relationships. It seemed every person he'd come to care about left him one way or another. He tightened his grip on Sophie's hand. He wasn't going to lose her.

Reece turned to see the movie's screenwriter heading his way. His gut tightened. No denying she was one good-looking lady, and he definitely needed to stay cool. She was Hollywood bound. A career woman. And after this movie, he was leaving Hollywood behind to make a home for Sophie. He released a long breath.

Life sure would be simpler if she was still only the pretty waitress at the Good Time Café....

Chapter Two

*Thanks to our neighbors, the barn is finally built.
And if the weather holds, I promised Becky I
would start the cabin. Although, she deserves to
live in a stately mansion, she said all she wants
is a home right here, with me.*
Jacob's Journal

"Why didn't you say you were associated with the movie?" Emily asked as she stood in front of the truck.

"I could ask you the same thing," Reece countered, helping Sophie drink some water. "Also why are you moonlighting as a waitress?"

"I was just helping out. Sam Price, the owner, is a family friend."

Before he could say anything else, Nate appeared behind her. "Tell the truth, sis," her brother began and looked at Reece. "Emily decided the set builders would finish faster if she made herself scarce."

"That's right. You and Shane didn't run me off, it was my decision to help Sam."

"And it was a good choice," Nate teased, then glanced down at the child. "We weren't expecting any of the crew for a few days, but Jason mentioned this morning that you might show up early to check out the terrain. Who's your friend?"

"My niece, Sophie," Reece said. "She recently came to live with me...permanently."

Nate knelt down to be eye level with her. "Hi, Sophie. I'm Emily's brother, Nate."

Emily watched as the child's eyes lowered shyly. The little girl's arm latched tighter on to her uncle's leg.

Emily's heart went out to the forlorn looking girl. It was obvious she'd been through some kind of trage- dy...but to lose both parents. She knew all too well what it felt like to lose someone you loved. Even after a dozen years, she still missed her father.

Emily shook away the memories and put on a smile. "Sophie, remember me?"

The child raised her eyes and nodded. Just that slight response tickled Emily. "How about you and I go up to the house and have some lemonade and cookies while your uncle tends to his horses?"

Emily looked at Reece for permission. "There's no need for you to feel you have to watch her." Reece said.

Emily took Sophie's hand. "Since I'm not needed at

the movie set until tomorrow, Sophie will be doing me a favor. And since you need to take care of those beautiful animals, your niece and I can entertain each other." She glanced at the child. "What do you say, Sophie? You want to go with me?"

Sophie turned her big brown eyes on her uncle and saw him nod. "It's okay. I'll come and get you just as soon as I care for Toby and Shadow."

Holding on to her raggedy bear with one hand, and with the other in Emily's, the two started off toward the house.

Reece watched them walk away. He should be happy that his niece was responding to someone. Except that it could be a problem. Sophie could get too attached, and their time in Haven was only going to be temporary. Reece remembered too well how much it hurt when he'd gotten too attached to a person when he was growing up. He couldn't stand that happening to Sophie.

"She'll be okay," Nate said.

Reece came out of his reverie. "What did you say?"

"I can assure you that my sister is good with kids. It's men she's been known to be hard on." A friendly grin appeared. "I guess my brother Shane and I had something to do with that. We used to tease her, but she gave back as good as she got."

Reece didn't want to hear about Emily Hunter's attributes. He had to stay focused on the reason he was here. The money he'd make would go a long way in helping him to achieve his goal of buying his own ranch.

Shadow whinnied and Reece returned to the present and his responsibilities. "Would you mind if I let the horses loose in your corral? It's been a long trip."

"Sure, let me help," Nate said as they walked to the animals. "I hear you're from California. Do you own a ranch there?"

He wished. "No, just an apartment in L.A. I board my horses out in Riverside." He'd worked out a deal with the ranch owner, Jerry Holt, to train horses in trade for boarding his black mare and bay gelding in between jobs.

Reece took Shadow by the reins and led him into the corral, while Nate brought Toby. Reece glanced around the freshly painted barn. "You've got a nice place here."

"Thanks." Nate closed the gate and removed the lead rope from the horse's bridle. "The Double H had been in the family for generations, but we'd lost it when our father died. I bought it back about ten months ago." A sudden sadness masked Nate's face. "It was shamefully run-down. My brother Shane, owns a construction company, and he's responsible for all this restoration work."

Reece released Shadow and the animal ran off. "I take it he's the one building the movie set?"

Nate nodded. "The producer is a stickler for detail, so we're replicating the original homestead."

Reece had worked for Jason before so he knew the man's desire for realism. He was anxious to see the location, but he also needed to get Sophie settled for the night.

"Do you know what the accommodations will be?"

Nate nodded. "The actors will have trailers. Jason and I have an agreement for the crew to stay in the new bunkhouse. There are five female crew members that will share the foreman's house."

"You're being pretty generous with your place."

Nate watched the horses gallop around in the sun. "I haven't exactly got the ranch up and running yet so I'm not using most of the facilities right now. At the moment I just have a small herd and a few saddle horses. My hope is to have things up and running by the spring. The truth is I'm not even sure how big an operation I want to handle, and if it will be cattle, or mostly horses."

Reece wouldn't have any trouble deciding at all. "If I had the money and a place like this, I'd do both, but I'd definitely breed horses."

Nate smiled. "My great-great-grandfather was a horse breeder. He had a line of champion stock that was well known around this area," he said. There was obvious pride in his voice.

"Must be nice to trace your family back so far," Reece said. Hell, he didn't even know his father.

"Damn straight. That's why it's only right the Hunter family story be told where it all began. For a while there, we'd lost everything, but we still had each other. That's the most important thing. I take it you're Sophie's only family."

Reece nodded. "Her mother died recently, and her father was never in the picture. I'm her guardian now." He didn't want to go into any more details. "And I need to talk to Jason. Is he around?"

Nate shook his head. "He flew to L.A. earlier this morning, but he'll be back Tuesday."

"Did he happen to mention about arrangements for a place for me?"

Nate's eyebrow drew together. "No, he didn't say anything to me."

"Damn, I was afraid of this. I can't work on the movie if I don't have a place for Sophie and me to stay, and someone to watch her while I work. Jason promised to help me out."

Nate raised a hand. "Let's not panic. I'm sure Jason has something in the works, but in the meantime, why don't you move into the bunkhouse. It's just sitting empty."

That wouldn't solve Reece's long-term problem, but he was grateful he and Sophie would have someplace to sleep that night. "You sure it's okay?"

Nate smiled. "It's my bunkhouse. So relax. Now, let's get out of this heat and go up to the house."

Reece hesitated, but ended up following Nate. He wasn't going to stay long. They'd spend the night, but there was a good chance that this job wasn't going to pan out. He glanced toward the mountain range. That was a shame. This sure was beautiful country.

In the ranch kitchen, Emily sat on the hardwood floor with Sophie. The child played silently, putting a dress on one of Emily's old dolls that they'd found in the attic. Emily tried to interact, but the little girl seemed more comfortable on her own.

"Too bad you're having a boy," Emily said, glancing up at her pregnant sister-in-law. "All these dolls are going to waste."

The petite blonde ran her hand over her protruding stomach. She was due in a couple of months. "We might just have a girl one day."

Emily studied her sister-in-law's smile. Nate and Tori were so happy, but that hadn't happened easily. Although Nate had fallen in love with the San Francisco heiress almost immediately, Tori had men issues, a dominating father and a bad relationship with a man who cared only about her money. Nate had changed all that. And even though she'd been raised in the city, Tori took to ranch life as if she were born into it.

"So, you're already thinking about another baby?"

Tori glanced at Sophie. "Who wouldn't want a child like this little one? She's beautiful."

The girl looked up. Her eyes showed her excitement as she held her doll up to Emily.

"Oh, what a good job you did dressing Sunny," she praised her. When the child didn't move the doll, she realized she was giving it back. "Sophie, you can keep her," she said.

There was a glimmer of joy on Sophie's face and Emily decided she'd do almost anything to see that look again. Just then the back door opened and Nate walked in along with Reece. Tori went to her husband and kissed him. Amazingly Emily found she wanted to go and greet the brooding man standing stiffly in the doorway. She told herself it was to see if she could get a reaction from him. Her gaze went to his mouth, wondering how it would feel to kiss him. She raised her eyes to his and heat rushed to her face.

It was Sophie who distracted them. She got up and ran to her uncle. She held up the doll and whispered his name. "Unca Reece. See? Her name is Sunny."

He looked confused. "She's pretty."

Nate brought his wife closer. "Tori, this is Reece McKellen, the stuntman on the movie. Reece, my wife, Tori. And she's carrying our son, Jake."

Reece removed his cowboy hat and nodded. "Nice to meet you, ma'am. And congratulations on the baby."

"Thank you. And please, call me Tori."

"I hope Sophie hasn't been too much trouble." He tossed a quick glance at Emily.

"Oh, no," Tori said. "She's been a joy. She's so well behaved."

Smiling, Nate placed a glass of iced tea on the counter for Reece. "And Tori should know about kids, she's taught school."

Reece liked the Hunters. They've graciously welcomed him and Sophie into their home, but it didn't change the fact that he always felt like an outsider. He hadn't fit in many places, especially ones like this. He glanced around the beautiful kitchen as he took a long drink of tea. Man, it was something. He admired the honey maple cabinets and dark granite counters. The hardwood floors gleamed with high-gloss polish.

There was a knock on the door. It opened and an older woman peeked inside the room. "Hi, I was in the neighborhood and thought I'd stop by."

"Mom, you don't need an excuse to come by," Nate said as he went to the woman and hugged her.

"She's here to check up on me," Emily began. "Sam called you, didn't he?"

The attractive older woman smiled innocently. "He may have mentioned that you didn't finish your shift." Mrs. Hunter glanced at Sophie. "Well, who do we have here?"

"Sorry, Mom," Emily began. "This is Sophie and her uncle, Reece McKellen. He is working on the movie. Reece, this is our mother, Betty Hunter."

Mrs. Hunter had short gray hair and a slender build. "Oh, my, you're one of the movie stars, aren't you?" she said. Her blue eyes, so much like her daughter's, widened.

Everyone laughed. "Sorry to disappoint you, ma'am, but I'm just part of the crew," he said.

"Reece is the stuntman on the movie," Nate offered.

"Oh, so you're doing Camden Peters's stunts."

"Yes, ma'am. A little trick riding."

"What happens if you get hurt?"

Reece couldn't help but smile. "I don't plan on that happening. I learned how to fall during my rodeo days. Believe me, those broncos have so many creative ways to toss you off, I'm pretty sure I've learned them all."

"Oh, I hope so." She glanced down at Sophie. "Is this your little girl?"

"My niece. She lives with me now."

Betty Hunter smiled. "Just look at all those beautiful curls. You remind me of Emily. She had hair like this. And she was such a precocious child."

Emily groaned. "Mother, I'm sure Mr. McKellen doesn't want to hear about my childhood."

Reece found he enjoyed Emily's blush. Damn, if it wasn't as appealing as the rest of her. He placed a hand on Sophie's shoulder. "I think it's time we get settled. Thank you, Nate, for your hospitality." He looked at Emily. "And thank you for watching Sophie. Would you happen to have Jason's cell phone number?"

"Sure." She went to the purse on the counter and searched the for a business card. She handed it to him. "Is there a problem?"

"Just a little mix-up with living arrangements." Reece didn't want to involve the Hunters in his problems. "Thanks again for watching Sophie."

"It was my pleasure," Emily said. "Bye, Sophie."

When he turned to the door, Nate stopped him. "I'll bring some bedding down to the bunkhouse later. Say, why don't you and Sophie come up for supper tonight? There's always plenty."

Reece knew Nate meant to be neighborly, but he hated feeling obliged to people. "Thank you, but we're both pretty tired after the long drive today."

Sophie started to hand back the doll and Emily came down on her knee. "Oh, sweetie, remember, I gave Sunny to you, to keep. Maybe we can play again." She touched the child's cheek. "See you later."

Reece saw the longing in his niece's eyes. He knew she was lonely, how much she'd missed her mother. And someone like Emily and her family would be easy to turn to, but he had to remember the stop at the Double

H was only temporary. He stole one last glance at Emily Hunter, knowing if he stayed the next few months were going to be full of temptation. For both of them.

At seven-thirty that evening Emily made her way toward the bunkhouse, all the time telling herself that she was only bringing them the bedding. She was not doing it because she wanted to see Reece McKellen again. Okay, so he was a drop-dead sexy man, who didn't seem to like her, she reminded herself. Why? Was he just not attracted to her? Okay, she could accept that. She shook her head. Why was she even thinking about him? She didn't need to get involved at this time in her life. Not with her career just taking off. She needed to stay focused on *Hunter's Haven*.

She'd worked too hard to get through school and spent too many hours on her feet as a waitress to let a man come along and turn her head now. But it wasn't just the man, it was Sophie. Emily was drawn to her, too. And that was even more dangerous. Just as soon as she dropped off the sheets and towels, she'd stay away from them both.

Emily stepped up on the wooden porch and glanced through the bare window. Sophie at the table playing with her new doll. Emily knocked, then opened the door.

"Hi, Sophie."

"Emily." The little girl stood up. All ready for bed, the child was wearing pink pajamas, her damp hair in ringlets.

Emily's heart tightened. "I brought you some towels and sheets." Just then she heard running water in the
other room. Well, she wasn't about to interrupt the
man's privacy to give him a towel.

She glanced around the ranch hand's new quarters
that Shane had built this past spring. The efficient kitch-
en had a stainless-steel stove, an oversize refrigerator
and a long table that could seat twenty men. On either
side of the room a hallway led to the two bedrooms. She
knew that the large bathroom was designed in two sections with several walk-in shower stalls, separate from
the sinks and toilets. She didn't want to think about the
naked man now using one of the stalls, or the water
spraying over his muscular body.

She quickly shook away the image and turned her
focus to the table holding a cooler and groceries. "Did
you eat?"

Sophie nodded.

Emily saw the carton milk and loaf of bread. Why
didn't they just come to the house and have pot roast?
No. That wasn't her business.

"Hey, how about I make up your bed? Where are you
sleeping?"

The child motioned for her to follow as she walked
into the nearest bedroom where five single bunks lined
both sides of the long walls. The first two had sleeping
bags opened on top of the new mattresses.

"I think I can make you a little more comfortable.
Emily pulled off one nylon bag and spread out the sheet.
"You want to help me?" Sophie came over, and with

some instruction, she tucked in the corners. Of course it wasn't as good as could be, but the child was obviously proud of her handiwork. With one bed made, Emily started on the other. Maybe if she hurried she'd be finished before Reece returned. Suddenly she glanced up and saw the man in the doorway, leaning lazily against the frame. Too late.

No fantasy she'd ever had came close to the real thing. The real thing was six foot two inches of pure male standing there in a pair of worn jeans and nothing else. His broad shoulders and well developed chest were bare and damp.

"Unca Reece," Sophie called out. "I made my bed."

"You sure did," he acknowledged never taking those sable eyes off Emily.

"Emily helped me," she said.

"I can see that," he told her. "You just seem to show up everywhere."

Emily felt heat flood her face. "Tori wanted to make sure you had enough bedding. I brought towels, but I can see you didn't need them."

"We made do, but thanks." He went to the other side of the bed and began to tuck in the sheet, careful to make sure that Sophie was able to help. "We're leaving in the morning and heading back to L.A."

"But the movie… Have you heard anything from Jason?"

She shook her head. "I've called, but he's been in meetings all day."

"I'm getting the same message. If I didn't have Sophie it wouldn't matter. But I need to provide her with a stable environment. Her caseworker wasn't crazy about me bringing her on location as it was."

Emily realized she didn't want to see them go, but knew the child had to come first. "What will Jason do about a stuntman?"

"It's not a problem to replace me. The stunts are pretty simple. A good horseman should be able to handle them. Even Camden Peters."

Emily shook her head. "It's stipulated in his contract that he doesn't do stunts."

Reece's face split into a grin and her breath caught. "I guess he's afraid to take any chances."

"I don't care. We're lucky to get him for the part."

Reece had worked with Camden Peters once before. The man was demanding and used his star power to get special treatment. "I'd say he's the lucky one to have a chance at such a great part."

Emily didn't know why, but this man's praise meant a lot to her. "Thank you." Her gaze lowered to see a series of faint scars across his chest. "Is that from one of your stunts?"

He didn't look down. "No, they're from my rodeo days," he said. "I guess I'm lucky I don't have to take off my shirt for my part in the film." There was a twinkle in his eye.

She swallowed. "I imagine my ancestors got a few scars settling this land. You'd look perfect, scars and all."

His mouth twitched in amusement. "I'll take that

as a compliment. But stuntmen get paid for their ability to make the actors look good. No one sees my face."

Oh, that was a shame. He wasn't pretty-boy handsome, but he had rugged good looks. Deep-set eyes that pierced right through you, a sharp jawline and a chin that displayed a deep cleft. But it was his mouth and a full bottom lip that, for the second time, made her wonder how it would feel against hers. Heat surged through her and she shook away the direction of her thoughts. "Well, I guess I should get back," she said, realizing she was getting too up close and personal with the man.

"Thanks for the sheets and towels."

"You're welcome." When she headed toward the door, he followed her. She reached for the doorknob and he did the same. Warmth shot up her arm and she jerked away just as Sophie came running to her, but stopped short and stood by her uncle's side.

Emily knelt down to the child's level. "You get some sleep. Sweet dreams."

Emily moved to the door, but made the mistake to look over her shoulder to see the two. *Just leave and don't get any more involved.* But it was too late.

She found herself saying, "I think I know a place you could live during the filming. My mother has a small apartment over the garage."

Reece McKellen's expression didn't change except for a slight rise of his eyebrow. Emily decided that was probably the most emotion he showed people. Well, that was just fine, especially since she'd see him nearly every day for the next few months. They would be working together.

"Are you interested?"

His dark eyes pierced hers. "I'm very interested."

Chapter Three

Thanks to our neighbors' help, the barn is finally built. And if the weather holds, I promised Becky I will start the cabin. Although, she deserves to live in a stately mansion, she said all she wants is a home, right here with me.
Jacob's Journal

The next morning at the ranch, Emily was up at 6:00 a.m. After a quick shower, she headed downstairs to find coffee and her brother. Since their father's death, she—as well as the rest of the family—had always turned to Nate with her problems. And he'd always been there for her. Not just financially to help her through college, but whenever she needed emotional support. He might have been a little heavy-handed when it came to prospective boyfriends, but when it came to important choices, like her deciding on a film career, he'd stood by her. And now she could use his reassurance. She was filling her mug when he walked in.

"Mornin', Em," he grumbled. Although he was showered and dressed for ranch work, his eyes were still heavy from sleep.

"Hi, Nate." She handed him her mug and poured another for herself.

"Thanks," he said and took a sip. "Tell me again why I want to be a rancher. These hours are worse than those of a sheriff."

She knew he wasn't serious. Her brother had spent the past dozen years working and saving to get the Double H back in the Hunter family. "You love the smell of horse manure in the morning?"

He tugged on her ponytail. "You've got a smart mouth." He took another sip and leaned against the counter. "It's going to get pretty busy around here in a few days. Are you sure you're ready for this?"

No! But she wanted it more than anything. "Are you kidding? You know I've been dreaming about all of this forever."

"Sometimes reality isn't as perfect as the dream."

Her pulse raced in panic. Nate and Shane had been working closely with Jason, from building the set to working out housing for the crew and corralling the animals. "Is there something you're not telling me?"

He shook his head. "No. I'm only saying the next few months are going to be hectic."

Emily knew she'd be working with a demanding director, Trent Justice, and didn't doubt she'd be doing rewrites for several scenes. "I can handle it. It's you and Tori I'm worried about. Are you sure this isn't too much for you guys? Especially Tori? You've shared your home, and now with a baby due in six weeks…"

"Tori is loving it. You know that she loves having people around. But if it gets too crazy, I'll keep her in the house," he said and laughed. "Yeah, as if she'd let me boss her around."

Everyone could see how much Nate and Tori were in love. Her other brother, Shane, had also married recently, and his wife, Mariah was the love of his life. They had sneaked off to Las Vegas and didn't tell a soul. They were excepting a child in the spring. It was hard not to envy what her brothers and their wives had.

"With all the commotion going on I hope it won't be a distraction from your work for the gallery?" she said. Nate, who was also a talented wood carver, had a show coming up.

He smiled. "Not if you don't mind waiting for me to replace the figurine I borrowed from you."

How sweet. When Nate's talent had first been recognized he needed several carvings for his initial show. That show's money had been what helped buy back the ranch. Friends and family donated their carvings to help the cause. She'd never regretted giving him the horse figurine he'd carved for her. "How about you give it to me for a wedding gift?"

Nate cocked an eyebrow. "Are you trying to tell me something?"

She laughed. "I'm telling you that you'll have plenty of time to replace my carving."

He studied her for a moment. "Be careful, someone just might walk through that door and you'll fall like a ton of bricks."

"Is that how it happened for you?" Tori asked from the doorway. She was wearing her gown and robe.

"Sure was." Smiling, Nate went to his wife. "I thought you were going to sleep in?"

"I was until junior decided to play a game of kick ball. I'll nap later." She looked at her sister-in-law. "How did you sleep in your old room?"

This was the house Emily had grown up in until their father died. When they couldn't pay the mortgage, the bank repossessed the property. "Great, but I can't impose on you guys anymore. You've done so much already."

Tori glanced from her husband to Emily. "I grew up in a big lonely house so I love having people around. You'll never be intruding." She wrapped her arm around her husband's waist. "We want the whole family to feel like this is their home, too."

Emily swallowed the lump in her throat and glanced at her brother. "I'm sure glad you were wise enough to marry her."

"So am I."

Emily watched as the two exchanged a look that showed the depth of their love. Lately, when both her brothers were with their wives, she'd felt like the fifth wheel, an intruder. But someday she hoped she'd find their happily-ever-after kind of love with a special guy.

There had been someone in college, but he wasn't willing to allow her time for her career. She'd spent too many years in school not to get a chance to prove herself. She preferred to think that the real reason she hadn't settled down was that she hadn't found the man of her dreams yet.

Suddenly the picture of a big, strong cowboy who'd been so tender with his niece popped into her mind. Not many men would single-handedly take on the responsibility of a child. But she doubted Reece McKellen was like most men.

There was a soft knock on the door. She watched as Nate went to answer it and found the man who'd plagued her thoughts most of the night standing there along with his niece. And he looked pretty dreamy in faded jeans and a black T-shirt.

"I know it's early, but I saw the light on."

"Not a problem. Come in," Nate said.

The child followed him inside. She was dressed in a pair of jean shorts and a blue cotton top with ruffles around the neck and sleeves. Her hair was pulled back in a slightly crooked ponytail. The little girl beamed when she saw her. Emily held out her hand and Sophie came to her.

"Good morning, Sophie. Are you hungry?"

The child nodded.

Nate handed Reece a cup of coffee. "Why don't you stay for breakfast," he said. "There's plenty."

"Thanks, but we were going to eat in town."

Reece watched as Emily escorted his niece to the table. He stiffened. He knew the invitation was a friendly gesture, but he needed to stay away from the warm family scene. To keep this strictly business. He also needed to stay clear of the attractive leggy brunette with the smile that got him stirred up. She had him aching, and not only with physical need. But the truth was he had all the commitment he could handle right now with Sophie.

Reece forced himself to make eye contact with Emily. "I stopped by to see if you talked to your mother?"

"Oh, right," she said. "Nate, do you think Mom would consider renting Reece the garage apartment?"

Her brother blinked. "I don't see why not, it's been empty since Shane and Mariah moved out." He looked back at Reece. "It's only a one-bedroom, but the sofa pulls out into a bed."

"Sounds good," Reece said. He hated to be indebted to the Hunters any more than he already was, but he didn't have a choice. "When will you be able to talk to your mother?"

"I'll call her now." Nate reached for the telephone on the wall. "She's usually finished with her run my now." He dialed his mother's number, then spoke into the phone.

"Hi, Mom." He paused. "No, Tori's okay. I just had a question about the garage apartment. How would you feel about renting it to Reece McKellen and his niece?" He paused again and listened. "Okay, fine. I'll talk to you later, Mom. Bye." He hung up and turned to Reece. "She only hesitated because it hasn't been painted in a while. She says it's not a problem, and you can come by any time to see it."

"That's great." Reece blew out a breath. "I still need to find someone to look after Sophie while I work, but this is certainly a start."

"You know, Mom might be able to help you with that, too," Nate said. "She runs the summer program at the elementary school. She might know of someone willing to baby-sit."

"Thanks. I'll need directions to the house."

"I'm headed there so you can follow me," Emily suggested.

He nodded. "Our stuff is all packed. So Sophie and I are ready whenever you are."

"That will be after breakfast," Tori told him. "Now everyone sit down while I make use of this great kitchen."

Reece reluctantly took a seat at the long trestle table and watched Emily take charge of Sophie. Under her guidance Sophie helped set the table. It wasn't long before scrambled eggs and bacon were put down in front of him. The easy, friendly conversation and laughter was uncomfortable for him. But not for Sophie. His niece responded as the two women fussed over her.

So much for keeping his interaction with the Hunters strictly business. The homey scene was a vision to him of what he'd and Carrie never had as children.

Finished with his breakfast, Reece got up and carried his plate to the sink.

"Help yourself to more coffee," Nate told him.

"Thanks, I've had plenty." He wanted to get going.

He glanced at Emily. They'd all finished eating, but no one seemed in a hurry to get on with the day. He'd never been good at small talk, he mused to himself.

Tori approached him. "You know, Reece, I'm going to be volunteering at the school this morning. If you wouldn't mind, I would love to take Sophie with me. There will be kids her age there. We'll be back here a little after noon."

He looked at his niece. "Do you want to go to the school with Mrs. Hunter?"

Her dark eyes widened and she nodded. "Yes."

He should be happy that she was beginning to trust people and he thought that he should encourage her to spend time with other children. "Okay." He turned back to Tori. "I'll go get her car seat."

"There's no need," Nate said. "We've bought several for our baby for every growth stage, zero to eighty pounds. I'll make sure the right one is in the car for Sophie."

Reece nodded, then glanced at Emily. "Then I'm ready to go whenever you are." That was a lie. He wasn't ready for any of this. This happy and welcoming family. As a kid, he'd moved around too much. As an adult, he'd learned to rely only on himself.

This cozy scene was definitely something he had to avoid during his stay here. He told himself it was to protect Sophie, but he didn't need to be constantly reminded of what he'd missed in his life.

"The place is small, but since it's only temporary you and Sophie should do okay." Emily pushed open the door to the apartment over the garage.

She stood back as Reece glanced around at the main room that consisted of a recliner and a sofa that faced a small television. He walked down the hall and peeked into the small bath, then into the bedroom with only enough space for a double bed.

He returned and took a glance toward the tiny kitchen. "I'll take it," he told her.

"You didn't even ask how much it is."

He cocked his eyebrow. "I have no doubt it'll be fair. Besides, your mother is doing me a favor. I don't expect she'd planned on renting this place."

"She's wants to help out on the movie, too. After all, it was my father who was the start of this whole project."

"How's that?"

Emily smiled at the memory. "Dad gave me Great-great-grandfather's journals. Once I started reading about Jacob and Rebecca's journey from Pennsylvania to homestead here, I had to tell the story. I started writing their story in high school, then rewrote it and rewrote it several times in college." She sighed. "The manuscript had been rejected by everybody in New York. That's when I wrote the screenplay. Then I found Jason and the rest is history…."

"It's got to seem worth it now, though."

She smiled proudly. "Oh, yeah. And I can't wait until we start filming." His gaze met hers and suddenly she felt warm. She glanced away. "I hope you and Sophie have enough room for your things. There's only one dresser."

Reece leaned against the kitchen counter and folded his arms across his well-developed chest. "Sophie and I didn't bring much with us."

Emily had a feeling Reece McKellen had a lot more baggage, of the emotional variety, than he would ever reveal—to anyone. She busied herself, pulling open a drawer to find dishcloths and towels. Next, she looked in the cupboard under the sink.

"Good." She stood up and quickly realized how close the kitchen quarters were. "There are plenty of cleaning supplies." She tried to draw in air, finding it difficult. His masculine scent, a combination of soap and shaving cream, was making her light-headed. His coffee-colored eyes were riveted on her, causing her heart to race, her body to warm. "There are towels and sheets in the hall cupboard."

He didn't step back from her. "We'll manage," he said.

"I just want you to be comfortable."

"I'd be sleeping in my rig or the bunkhouse if it wasn't for Sophie. She's my biggest concern."

Emily saw in his expression the genuine love he had for his niece. "I can tell." There was a long pause, then Emily asked, "How long has Sophie's mother been...gone?"

"Just a month."

"Oh, my, I'm so sorry. Were you close?"

He shook his head. "No, I hadn't seen Carrie in years. We were separated when we were kids."

She decided it was best not to ask any more. "Oh, that's a shame. At least Sophie has you."

He glanced at Emily. "Oh, I don't know. I'm not sure I'm the best person for the job of raising a child."

She found she wanted to reach out to this man. She wanted to help him with some of the burden. "Your sister must have thought so. And I can see how much you care about Sophie, and how much she cares about you."

A sadness flashed in his eyes. Something tightened in her chest and she realized it had been a long time since she'd been attracted to a man. But this wasn't the time to start up a romance. Even a short-lived one.

"Hello," her mother's voice rang out. Smiling, Betty Hunter walked though the door with Sophie in hand. "See, I told you he was here."

Reece saw the worried look on his niece's face. Then she smiled at him and his heart felt a jolt. She hurried to his side and grabbed his hand.

"Did you have a good time?" he asked.

She nodded. "They have lots and lots of books."

"She did really well, at first," Betty said. "But the new surroundings and all the kids were a little overwhelming. And we're still strangers to her. That, combined with being away from you, made her a little anxious. So I told her I'd bring her to you."

"Thank you," he said.

"You're welcome. Children need their parents when they feel scared or insecure. Sophie has met a lot of strangers in the past two days. You're her reassurance."

"I'm new at this," he admitted. "I've only had Sophie for a short time. I wasn't sure that I should take this location job, but I have to make a living. That brings up my current problem. I need a sitter."

"I may have a solution," Betty began. "The summer

program runs from seven-thirty to noon for kids between four and twelve. I also talked with one of our high
school students, Tracy Perkins. I've known her family
for years. She's interested in watching Sophie during
the afternoons until the end of summer. You can drop
her off at school in the morning, and I can bring her
back here for Tracy."

Reece liked the idea, but there were still complications. "There'll be days when they want me on the set
before sunrise."

Betty didn't hesitate before she said, "Then you can
bring her to my house, and I can take her to the school
when I go."

Reece knew he didn't have a choice in this. He had
to have someone to watch Sophie and this kind woman was making it easy for him. "Mrs. Hunter, this would
be asking a lot of you."

"Please, call me Betty. If you were asking too much,
I'd tell you." She looked him in the eyes. "I know how
hard it is to raise a child on your own. And how important it is for you, as her caregiver, to know she's well
taken care of. I had to have help after my husband died.
There's no shame in asking for help."

"Hey, Em!" a male voice called from outside. "Are
you up there?"

Reece watched as a large man walked in the door. He
had dark hair and the same eyes as Emily. No doubt this
was the other brother. He gave a glance toward Reece,
then turned to his sister. "Hey, why didn't you answer me?

"I was hoping you'd go away," Emily teased. "You

know like yesterday at the site when you didn't want me around?"

"Come on, you know I was just teasing you." He went to her and drew her into a big hug. "I know you were just worried about us getting everything done in time," he said with a grin. "And admit it, you had fun working for Sam."

"Okay, I did. But did you get the cabin finished?"

"Now, I'm wounded." He place a hand over his heart. "Have I ever let you down?"

Emily mouth twitched. "Yes, there was that time when I was in third grade…"

Her brother laughed. "Isn't that just like a woman, they never let you forget." He turned to Reece. "Hi, you must be Reece McKellen. I'm, Emily's brother, Shane." He held out his hand and Reece shook it.

"Nice to meet you."

"Hi, Mom," Shane said, then leaned down and smiled at Sophie. "Who's your friend? Aren't you a cutie pie."

Surprisingly his niece smiled shyly.

"This is Sophie Rose," Betty announced.

"And just as pretty as a rose. I'm Shane."

"Isn't Sophie a little young, even for you?" Emily teased.

"No woman is too young for attention," he returned. "Besides I'm practicing for our little girl."

"You found out the sex of the baby?" Betty asked.

Shane shook his head. "Mariah isn't sure she wants to know, but I'm convinced it's a girl."

Reece looked at Emily as she explained. "Shane's wife, Mariah, is expecting a baby early next spring."

Shane grinned. "Yeah, be careful. I think it's something in the water."

Emily's face immediately reddened. "Shane. I'm sure you have a good reason for coming all the way into town."

"Oh, yeah. Nate said to tell you that a man named Camden Peters is at the ranch."

"Camden Peters!" Emily and Betty Hunter spoke at the same time.

"Yeah," Shane said. "And he wants to see the person in charge. Something about suitable accommodations."

Her brother nodded. "And he wants to see the person in charge. Something about accommodations."

Emily gasped. "Oh, no, I've got to get back." She rushed to the door.

"Oh, he's so handsome," Betty gushed. "I'd better go with her." She hurried after her daughter, then paused. "Oh, Reece. If you want the apartment, move in any time. We can work out the details later. Bye."

Shane just shook his head. "Hey, I don't know what the big deal is, Peters looks like a regular guy to me, except he has this cocky attitude. Women go for that?"

Reece shrugged. "He's a big box office draw. And he can make or break this movie." Reece didn't like to admit that. But he'd been around a lot of actors and their egos, and if they were in demand, they pretty much got their way and women's attention.

Shane grinned. "Then I think we better get out to the ranch and see if we can help keep things under control."

* * *

When Emily reached the house, she saw the town car in the circular driveway. She jumped out of the truck and ran up the steps and through the front door. Her mother was close behind her.

Camden Peters, with his thick brown hair and steel-gray eyes, was seated in the parlor in the wing chair that had been reupholstered when Tori redecorated the house.

The room was bustling with no less than four other people she didn't know. They were all taking instructions from the handsome actor so she figured Camden had brought them with him.

Emily's back straightened. Her daddy had taught her that the only way to face a scary situation was head-on. She walked into the room. "Hello, Mr. Peters." She continued toward his chair. "Welcome to the Double H."

The actor stood. He was tall, dressed in tapered western shirt, jeans and snakeskin boots. All looked brand-new.

"Well, suddenly things are beginning to look a little more pleasant," Peters said. "And you are…"

Suddenly it seemed hard to remember. "I… I'm Emily Hunter. I wrote *Hunter's Haven*."

"This is a pleasure," he said, taking her hand in his. "You're a very talented woman, Emily. I'm honored to play Jacob Hunter."

She hoped he meant that. "And we're very happy you've taken the part. But we weren't expecting you for a few days."

"I like to arrive on location early to get the feel of the place. It helps to get me into character." His mesmerizing gaze locked with hers. "I want to do justice to your story."

"I have no doubt you will," she said. It was obvious that he was flirting with her. Heaven help her. Just then Nate and Tori came in from the kitchen and her mother joined them.

"Mr. Peters," Nate said stepping forward. "This is my mother, Betty Hunter."

Camden took her mother's hand. "Mrs. Hunter, it's a pleasure."

"It's nice to meet you," she said. "I must say the entire town is excited to have you here for the movie."

"Why, thank you. It's good to finally start this project."

Nate put his arm around Tori and announced, "My wife and I would like to extend an invitation to you and your friends to stay for lunch."

"I'll look forward to it." He glanced at Emily. "If it's not too much trouble, I would like to ride out to the location site first. Then I'll need to find a place to stay until my trailer arrives. Can you direct me to a hotel in the area?"

Emily was about to tell him about the Desert Inn Motel when Tori spoke up, "Mr. Peters, we would be honored if you'd be our houseguest until then."

Emily could see by Nate's surprised expression that his wife hadn't talked it over with him beforehand. But her brother covered nicely. "Sure," he agreed. "We have plenty of room. And of course, the rest of your people are welcome to stay in the new bunkhouse."

"How can I turn down such a gracious invitation?" Peters said as he gave instructions to one of the men in the group to bring in his things and take them to the offered room.

Emily knew that Nate hadn't signed on for this. She needed to call Jason and let him know he'd better get back here and soon.

She put a smile on her face when Camden looked at her. "Are you ready to go for that ride?" he asked.

Emily was also eager to see the finished movie set. "Sure. I can take you out." She glanced at her sister-in-law. "Why don't we plan to go out after lunch?"

"Whenever it's convenient for Mr. Peters."

He smiled and leaned closer to Tori. "Since we're all going to be working so closely, just call me Camden."

Emily rode one of her brother's saddle horses, Maggie, while Camden was on Scout. The actor seemed more than capable of handling the large gelding. He sat easy in the saddle. The biography on him had stated he was from Texas. She could tell that he knew what he was doing as he maneuvered his horse through the rough terrain.

This area of the ranch hadn't seen many vehicles. It was part of the valley that seemed untouched by time. The site was beautiful. Exactly like what she'd always pictured when her great-great-grandfather Jacob Hunter had built the rough log cabin and barn for his horses and mule. Even the small corral had been reproduced down to the finest details.

"So this is the haven your ancestor settled," Camden said, breaking into her thoughts.

"This isn't the original homestead, but it's not far away." She pointed toward the ridge. "The same creek runs by each site," she said, looking toward the rocky stream.

Camden removed the straw hat that he'd borrowed from Nate and leaned back in the saddle. He sighed. "This place is beautiful. It's going to look great on film."

Emily was proud of her heritage, even after the years of heartbreaks and struggles. Back at the beginning of the twentieth century Jacob Hunter dreamed of owning his own land, a place to raise his family. "According to Jacob Hunter's journal, both he and Rebecca fell in love with it here."

Camden climbed off his mount and came to her. "And your great-great-grandmother Rebecca called it a haven. *Hunter's Haven.*"

Emily smiled as she started to swing her leg over the horse, and was surprised when Camden reached up and encircled her waist. "I can manage," she said, but he didn't release her.

"I'm just trying to be a gentleman."

It had been a long time since a man has helped her do anything. She also knew Camden Peter's reputation with the ladies. She finally made it to the ground and quickly stepped away. The horse suddenly shifted and pushed her back into Camden. He gave her that sexy grin that he was famous for. Maybe she should be flattered by his attention, but all she wanted was this man to star in her movie, nothing more.

She finally regained her balance just as a rider approached them. Great. She recognized both the horse and rider.

It was Reece.

He pulled up next to them and leaned an arm on the saddle horn. "Nice afternoon for a ride."

Camden released Emily. "We thought so. What are you doing here, McKellen?"

Reece swung his leg over the horse and jumped to the ground. "I'm here to deliver a message," he said.

Emily quickly moved away from the actor. "Reece, is there a problem?"

"No, Jason is back," he told her, then glanced out toward the valley. "Along with some of the crew, equipment and the trailers. It's a little hectic back at the house. And he wants to meet with both of you."

"Good, I want to talk with him, too," Camden said as he got on his horse.

Emily could barely control her excitement as she climbed back into the saddle. It was truly going to happen. Her dream of Hunter's Haven being made into a movie was starting to come together.

Chapter Four

Tonight as I gaze at the millions of stars in the prairie sky and listen to lowing cattle, all I can think about is my Becky back at the cabin. I close my eyes and see her smile, hear her voice, feel her touch. She's the reason I keep going... the reason I want a make a home and a life here.
Jacob's Journal

Angry with himself, Reece tugged on the rein and headed his horse in the direction of the ranch. He had no right to be possessive over Emily Hunter. No right whatsoever. That did stop him from feeling jealous, though, or keep him from admiring her as she rode off. She was a natural in the saddle and handled her horse with ease. Of course, she'd grown up on a ranch.

Too bad she'd given it all up for Hollywood.

Reece pressed his heels into Toby's ribs and the horse took off to catch up with the twosome, but he held back. Peters wasn't happy with him for breaking up the cozy scene. As if he cared.

Camden Peters had a reputation with women. Not that Emily was naïve, but after Nate had mentioned how starstuck she was over this man, he knew he had to check out the situation. What he hadn't expected was how protective he'd felt toward the screenwriter. The main thing that he had to remember was that this was just another job—his last in this business.

When they arrived back at the corral, Reece climbed down and went over to the other riders. "I'll take the horses," he said and reached for the reins.

"I can take care of my own mount," Emily said.

That's when Peters stepped in. "Let McKellen do his job, Emily. We can't keep Jason waiting."

Reece refused to let Peters get to him. "Yeah, go on, Jason is in the bunkhouse. I'll handle things here."

"Come on, sweetheart," Camden said, and took her arm and led her away.

Emily could handle Camden's God's-gift-to-women act, but she wasn't sure how to deal with the friction between Camden and Reece. Great. She didn't need this.

"Thank you," she called to Reece. He nodded and led the horses toward the barn.

Irritated, Emily eased from Camden's hold, and marched toward the newly constructed bungalow, her long strides easily eating up the distance. She took the time to watch the trailers being parked along the far side of the barn. There were also several equipment trucks and generators. She smiled. Things were finally moving along.

She hopped up onto the bunkhouse porch and stepped inside to see Jason seated at the table. The young producer's shaggy blond hair hung over his forehead as he worked at his laptop computer. After finishing his task, he looked up and smiled.

"Emily, Camden," he said and stood and crossed to them. "It's good see you. And Camden, I'm sorry I wasn't here to meet you when you arrived."

"Not a problem. Emily and her family have made me feel more than welcome."

"I hear you were checking out the location," he said. "What do you think?"

"I think it looks great, very authentic," the actor said.

Jason nodded. "Emily's brothers did an incredible job of duplicating the original homestead. And thanks to their work, we're ready to start filming sooner than expected."

Camden frowned. "How soon?"

"As you've probably already seen most of the equipment has arrived. The on-site trailers should be set up by nightfall. So you'll have your own place."

Jason turned back to her. "Have you had a chance to show Reece around the site?"

"He came out to get us, but he didn't have much of a chance to look around."

Camden stepped in. "Wouldn't her brother, Nate, be available to do it?"

Jason shook his head. "We can't keep imposing on Emily's family. We've already gotten the use of the ranch. Shane built our main set, and Nate got the town council to okay the use of the historical downtown area. So it's time we left the Hunter family alone."

Emily knew that Nate and Tori had been happy to help out, but her brother also needed some free time to work on his carvings.

"Emily," Jason began. "Will you take Reece out to the site in the morning so he can check out the terrain for his stunts?" At her nod he continued, "Good, I want all the prep work wrapped up in a few days while the crew is setting up the equipment. The gaffer is flying in from L.A. tomorrow, along with Trent Justice."

There was an almost reverent tone in Jason's voice as he talked about the movie's director. Trent was young, but his first movie had been reviewed as creative and brilliant. He was also a friend of Jason's, and when he'd read *Hunter's Haven*, he'd been eager to do the movie.

"I can't wait to meet him," Emily said.

"Well, there won't be much time to socialize because I've moved up the film's starting date."

Emily felt another rush of excitement. "Will everything be ready?"

Jason just nodded. "Camden, I'd like you to read over the first couple of scenes," he said. "If you have any problems, you can discuss any changes with Trent."

The actor nodded. "If that's all, I'll head up to the house. Are you coming, Emily?"

"I want to ask Jason a couple of things. You go on."

After Camden left, she turned to Jason. "Is everything really okay?"

He smiled. "Why wouldn't it be?"

"Well, maybe because you flew out of here two days ago and didn't tell a soul."

"I just had some business to tie up in L.A."

Her heart sank. "Jason, did we lose backing?"

He frowned. "No, and we're still above the line. But any downtime will eat into our limited funds. That's why I've decided to move up the start time, to save money."

She wasn't convinced. "If you need money, I still have—"

He waved her off. "No, you've invested more than enough, and your family isn't taking a penny for the use of the ranch. I knew getting Camden Peters would cost us—but he's worth it. His name is going to get us the distribution we'll need to make this film a success." He frowned. "Emily, I know he can be demanding, but he's a good actor. And he can make this movie a hit."

"Then we'll keep him happy. When are Jennifer Tate and the rest of the actors scheduled to arrive?"

"Jennifer just finished a film in Canada. She should be here tomorrow, the next day at the latest." He smiled. "I've worked with Jenny before, and she'll have no problem getting up to speed."

Emily clasped her hands. "Oh, I can't wait."

Jason hugged her. "You have a right to be excited. You wrote a great screenplay, Emily."

Again, she thought of her father. She'd never missed him so much as she had at this moment.

Oh, Dad, I wish you were here to share it with me.

Later that afternoon, Reece was busy tending to the horses. He needed to catch up from the time he'd lost settling into the apartment and getting Sophie registered in preschool. Now, he had to focus on his job and the care of the animals since he was also the wrangler on the movie.

Reece stroked the grooming brush over Toby's flank and the gelding blew out a breath. "You like that, fella?" Reece worked harder at his task. "I guess I've neglected you lately. I've been a little busy. Sophie's been taking most of my time. Not that I mind, but who would have thought that such a tiny little thing could turn a guy's life upside down? But she's worth it. I just need to find the rhythm to this sudden parenthood. And a way to make her happy again."

Betty Hunter had been right. He did need help caring for his niece. Although he hadn't wanted to ask, he didn't have much of a choice. Like when Tori had offered to watch her while he'd ridden out to find Emily.

Right now, Sophie was napping up in Emily's old bedroom. The biggest concern he had was that his niece would get used to this place having everyone around and being part of a big family. That was something he couldn't provide for her. There would be only the two of them.

Reece pushed aside a pang of loneliness as he ran the

brush over the quarter horse's back several more times, then stopped. "Okay, that should hold you for a while. I need to see Shadow." Toby bobbed his head. "What can I say? She needs her share of attention to."

He walked out of the stall, closed the gate, and then made his way down to Shadow's pen. But the mare wasn't alone. Emily Hunter was busy grooming her. Dressed in worn jeans that hugged her long legs and shapely bottom, the woman made a tempting picture. He blew out a breath, and raised his gaze to her chambray blouse. The top two buttons were open, exposing her long slender neck. Feeling his body stir, he jerked his attention to the horse.

"What are you doing?" he asked.

"I thought I was brushing Shadow." She paused and smiled. "Maybe I'm doing it wrong."

Damn. Why did she have to smile at him? How was he supposed to concentrate when she did that? "You're doing it fine. It's just not your job," he said as he stepped into the stall. It was close quarters with the large mare taking up most of the space.

"I like grooming horses," she said. "It was one of the chores I did as a kid." She worked the hard-bristled brush along the horse's back. "It was also one of my favorites. Besides, Shadow and I are getting to know each other."

He stroked the mare's neck. "She telling you any secrets?"

Emily nodded and her ponytail bobbed. "Could be. Lucky for me, since you're not an easy man to read, Mr.

McKellen, but I've discovered one thing. You do have a special way with animals and children."

Reece was mesmerized by her incredible eyes. "Maybe they're just easier to get along with."

She shrugged. "Maybe, but I don't think you let anyone get close enough to find out."

He didn't like the way she seemed to see inside him, or the pull of attraction he felt whenever she was around. Yet he couldn't seem to resist it.

He reached for her, and when she didn't resist, he pulled her to him. "We seem to be pretty close right now."

This man drove Emily crazy. He was purposely trying to scare her off. But it wasn't his actions that bothered her, but the way he set her heart pounding. She tried to come up with reasons why this was a bad idea. Why being in Reece McKellen's arms could be disastrous. But curiosity and desire got the best of her. "Yeah, we are. What are you going to do about it?"

She thought she'd pushed too far when she felt his sudden ragged breath against her face, and the strength of his arms around her. His deep-set gaze held hers for what seemed like forever, then his mouth lowered to hers. Automatically her lips parted in anticipation of his kiss.

"Emily!"

On hearing Nate's voice, Reece released her and she moved back. "I'm here, Nate," she answered, trying to keep her voice from trembling.

Smiling, her brother came down the center aisle,

leading little Sophie. She was wearing her jean shorts and cotton shirt, but on her feet were a pair of tiny black cowboy boots. Emily grinned, recalling they'd been hers when she was about Sophie's age. Her mother must have saved them. "Hey, who's the cowgirl?"

"Hi, Emily, Unca Reece," she called. "I got cowboy boots."

Reece looked over the stall railing. "I can see that."

"Our mother found an old pair of Emily's," Nate explained. "She thought that Sophie might like them."

He nodded. "Thank you."

Nate looked at his sister. "Hey, if you want to work, you can muck out a few stalls."

"I'll pass, thank you," she said, gathering her grooming tools. "What's up?"

"We're barbecuing tonight, and Mom's handling the trimmings." He glanced at Reece. "And she told me that I was to invite you and Sophie—and not to take no for an answer."

Emily watched as Reece hesitated, then he finally nodded. "I'll take Sophie to clean up in the bunkhouse."

"Sorry, you can't take away my mom's best kitchen helper. They've been baking pies. Right, Sophie?"

She bobbed her head. "I'm helping Miss Betty make apple pie. Can I go back and help some more?"

Reece glanced at Nate. "I just don't want her to get underfoot."

"Are you kidding? My wife and mother are having a ball and so is Sophie. Why don't you get cleaned up and come up in about thirty minutes? But I warn you, they'll put you to work. I've got to go and set up the bar-becue. Come on, Sophie."

Emily saw Reece's concerned look as he watched the two walk away. "You don't need to worry about Sophie."

"Yes, I do. She's my responsibility. I can't let your family do it all."

"It's not as if you left her on the street. You have to work. You're not neglecting her."

"And I don't want her to think I am." She saw something flash in his eyes. "Sophie hasn't exactly had the picture-perfect life…."

Emily wanted to hear more, but she wasn't going to push. "Then I guess she needs a good dose of family."

Reece took off his hat and ran a hand through his thick hair. "Maybe, but I don't want her to get too at-tached to your family, either. We're only here for a few months, then we have to leave." His gaze lingered a long time. "I have some plans and I can't let anything dis-tract me from them," he said.

Emily knew that remark was directed at her. "I can as-sure you Mr. McKellen, I'm not trying to distract anyone. My utmost concern the next three months is this movie."

With the last of her dignity, Emily marched out of the stall, angry with herself for even having given Reece an explanation. Darn it, if she wasn't attracted to the man. And there didn't seem she could do anything about it.

Reece sat with the Hunter family at the big table on the patio, watching as they laughed and teased each other.

Nate was next to his wife, Tori, and he couldn't stop looking at the petite blonde. It was the same with Shane and his pretty redheaded wife, Mariah. The newlyweds had been more obvious about their feelings, their touching and kissing almost shameless. Shane had his hands on his wife at every possible opportunity.

Camden Peters had his own audience with Betty Hunter. And that was all the actor needed. Next to her sat Sam Price, whose body language said that he disliked Peters acting so familiar with Betty.

Reece's gaze moved along the table to Emily who sat with his niece. The pretty brunette's attention was shared between Sophie and Jason Michaels. Did she and Jason have more than a working relationship? They seemed comfortable together. Was it possible for a man and woman to be just friends?

"Sophie is a beautiful child, Reece," Mariah Hunter said, interrupting his thoughts. "She must be a joy to you."

"Thank you. Yes, she is." He glanced at his niece. She was smiling. "I'm still trying to get used to parenthood."

Shane pulled his wife closer. "I can't wait," he said as he winked at her. The love between them was so intense, Reece had to look away.

He wanted to leave, but he couldn't take Sophie away just yet. He stole another glance at Emily while she helped the child cut her pie. The look between them was so tender, his chest tightened. He tried to push aside the feelings, but not before the picture of them as a family stampeded through his head. His niece had already stolen a piece of his heart. The last thing he needed was losing the rest to one pretty brunette who might do the same if he gave her half a chance.

It wasn't going to happen. Reece couldn't let it. He got up from the table, walked to the edge of the patio and leaned against one the posts just in time to see the sun heading behind the mountain range. The orange and yellow glow was so perfect it looked like a painting.

"It's pretty amazing, isn't it?" Nate said.

Reece didn't turn away from the sunset. "Yeah, it's pretty country, all right."

"Coming from a Texan, that's quite a compliment."

Reece had to smile. "I was born in Texas, but I've lived a lot of places, including California. I just can't afford to buy land there. Texas property just seems to be priced more reasonable."

"So you have your eye on a place there?"

Reece nodded. "It still costs more than I have, and the place needs a lot of work."

"The cattle business can be rough. We never know where the prices will go."

"I'm thinking about raising horses. There's always a need for good saddle mounts," Reece said. "Eventually I'd like to train cutting and reining horses."

"I'm surprised you aren't going to train horses for the movies."

The thought had crossed his mind. "Most riding these days is done in fast cars. Besides, I want out of the fast pace of Hollywood. I want Sophie to have a more stable life."

"Yeah, I want the same for my son." Nate glanced around. "I didn't know it at the time I got this ranch back, but I wouldn't change the peace and quiet of this place for anything. Of course, the woman I'm married to had a lot to do with my thinking. A home isn't a home unless you have the right person to share it with."

Reece thought about Emily. How had she been able to give this up? "I bet you worry about Emily being off in L.A."

Nate smiled. "I would worry about Emily no matter where she was. She's always been headstrong. But I give her credit for going after what she wants." He turned and stared at Reece. "My biggest concern is her happiness."

An hour later the party wound down. Emily smiled at the little girl with her head in her lap. Sound asleep. She stroked her fingers across Sophie's downy soft cheek and a strong yearning stirred in her. In just two days the child had managed to claim a permanent home in her heart.

Emily looked up and saw Reece standing across the patio. The intensity in his eyes tugged at her in a totally different way. Her chest tightened as she worked to draw air into her lungs, but she couldn't seem to look away. He started toward her, in a slow easy gait no woman could resist. He stopped in front of her, then crouched down and brushed a curl from Sophie's cheek. The tenderness she saw on his face, nearly brought tears to her eyes. She quickly blinked them away.

"Looks like she's out for the night." His eyes raised to meet hers. "I guess she had a pretty busy day." He tossed her a smile.

"Yeah, she did. All the partying will take it out of you."

Then to her surprise, his smile turned to a grin. Darn, the man was too handsome for his own good—and hers.

"I was thinking that it would be easier if she just stayed here tonight. She can sleep in my room."

"I can't put you out," he said.

"You're not. The bed's big enough for two," she said and felt her face redden. What was wrong with her?

"She doesn't have any clean clothes," he said.

"Neither do I. After she's in bed, I was going to drive to town. If you want I can get Sophie some clothes for tomorrow, too."

He released a breath and she could feel it against her skin. "I guess her staying here is better than waking her up to take her back to the apartment."

Emily nodded. "If you carry her upstairs, I'll go ahead and ready the bed."

Reece slipped his hands between the child and Emily. She tried not to notice his touch against her thighs as he worked her hands under the child. There was another brush against her stomach.

"Sorry," he breathed.

Finally the child's weight was lifted off her. Emily stood, and started for the house, Reece following behind. They went through the kitchen and up the back staircase. She hurried down the hall and opened the door to her old room, now painted a soft yellow. She jerked the floral comforter down along with the buttery top sheet.

She stepped back so Reece could deposit Sophie's head on the pillow. He pulled off the child's cowboy boots and set them on the floor. Emily stepped in and unfastened the snap to the tiny jean shorts and slipped them off revealing a pair of underpants decorated with flowers.

She quickly covered Sophie as she opened her eyes. She smiled, then curled to her side. "Night, Unca Reece...Emily."

"Night, sweetie," Reece said.

"Good night, Sophie," Emily said, then led Reece into the hall.

"If I didn't know better, I'd think she'd had this planned," Reece said.

Emily smiled. "Smart girl." She turned and headed for the stairs with Reece behind her.

Reece decided he might as well stay in the bunkhouse tonight, so he drove Emily back to town in his truck. They hadn't done much talking unless it concerned Sophie.

At the apartment, he packed his stuff, but was still gathering Sophie's clothes when Emily showed up at the door. "Come in," he called to her.

She hesitated in the bedroom doorway as he continued to rummage through the dresser. "I can't seem to find any underwear for Sophie."

"They're so tiny, you've probably just missed them." She walked over and started going through the other side of the dresser. Finally she held up another pair of flowery panties.

"Good. I guess I should just buy her more…of everything."

"Or maybe you should do laundry more often."

He snatched the pair from her hands. "It's bad enough I had to shop for her. I know nothing about little girls."

"If you want, I can help. There's a children's store in town."

"I don't think I'll have much time to shop."

"What a typical thing for man would say. If it were a truck or something electronic, you'd make the time."

"Those are important things. Clothes aren't."

"Maybe not to you, but to a girl they are." She jammed her hands against her hips. "So don't be stubborn about this. I'm only offering to help."

Emily sure looked good dressed in black jeans and a Western blouse and boots. He liked her hair down, brushing against her shoulders, looking a little wild. He couldn't stop thinking about when they were in the barn, when he'd pulled her into his arms. How good she'd fit against him.

He moved closer to her, inhaling her soft scent. "Seems like you're also offering something else…."

His challenging gaze met hers. She didn't back down. He reached for her, drawing her to him. "Seems we've been dancing around each other for a while now. May-

be it's time to discover if there's more than sparks between us. If you want to stop me, you better speak up
now."

When she didn't say anything, Reece lowered his
head and covered her mouth with his.

Chapter Five

Our first summer here has been hot and dry, so the coming of rain was a welcome relief. Becky's garden is thriving and so are the cattle. I've finished the cabin so we are cozy and warm, but after two weeks of constant rain, I'm wondering when it will stop.
Jacob's Journal

Emily had wanted Reece to kiss her since the moment he'd walked into the café. She just hadn't expected it to be the kind that made her heart pound, and her knees go weak. He pulled her into his arms, holding her close, pressing his lips against hers as if he had no intention of ending their kiss any time soon.

He broke away momentarily. Then he kissed her

again, longer, deeper, sweeping his tongue into her mouth and tasting her thoroughly. His hold tightened. She felt his hands slide down her back, the taut muscles of his thighs against hers. She whimpered as she wrapped her arms around his neck. Never had a man make her feel like this.

Reece pulled away, drawing a deep breath and releasing it. "Damn," he breathed.

Embarrassed, Emily stepped back. "I guess that wasn't such a good idea."

He raked his fingers through his hair. He looked as shaken as she felt. Good.

"May...maybe we should just forget this happened."

His dark eyes glared at her momentarily. "That's fine with me," he said. He turned to the bed and began to stuff the rest of the clothes into the duffel bag.

She stood there, still reeling from his kiss. "I mean we shouldn't start something we both know can't go anywhere."

He zipped up the bag and turned around. "We better get back."

She couldn't decide if she wanted to smack his stubborn jaw, or run back into his arms and kiss the daylights out of him.

"So we agree?"

He cocked an eyebrow. "I got the message, but actually, I'm not the man you should worry about," he said.

Another man? What other man? Then it suddenly dawned on her. "Are you talking about Camden Peters?"

Reece glanced at her.

"He just arrived today."

"Look, I want this job and the money it pays me. I've worked with Peters before and he's got a reputation for starting up romances while on location."

"Well, you can't blame only him," she said defensively. "He had to have had willing partners."

"Usually the women are too starstruck to realize what's happening. Just be careful."

Did he really think that after the way she'd kissed him that she could just go off to another man? It would serve him right if she did. "Thanks for the warning, but I'm not as naïve as you think. And believe me, I don't need another brother to protect me."

He stopped what he was doing. "Darlin' the last thing I'm feeling toward you is brotherly."

The next morning Reece was up early, or maybe he should say he hadn't slept more than a few hours. His bed in the bunkhouse wasn't the problem, Emily Hunter was. Most of the night he'd kept replaying their kiss.

After he'd fed Shadow and Toby and helped the workers around the barn to kill time, he finally headed up to the house. He needed to get Sophie and he needed to face Emily.

He climbed the steps to the back porch, but before he could knock, his niece opened the door. "Hi, Unca Reece." A smile transformed her face and her eyes rounded with excitement. "Emily said you would be here soon."

"Well, good morning, sweetie." He swung her up into his arms. She was dressed in the blue jeans and pink shirt he'd brought for her. And the cowboy boots. "So you didn't miss me last night?"

She sobered. "I missed you, but I wasn't scared. I got to sleep with Emily. And when I woke up we took a shower and she made my hair pretty."

"She sure did. That's one fancy braid." Reece tried hard to push aside the picture of a sleepy-looking Emily curled up in the big bed without success. "But you know that tonight you have to sleep in your own bed."

Sophie's mouth formed a pout, making her look amazingly like her mother. "I know, but... Can I stay here again? I like this house."

He was about to tell her it wasn't such a good idea when Emily walked into the kitchen. With a rush of pleasure he just looked at her. She was dressed in a blue Western shirt tucked into slim-fitting jeans. Her brown hair was pulled back in a long braid, just like Sophie's.

His gaze returned to her sleepy-eyed look, reminding him how long it had been since he'd shared a morning with a woman.

"Mornin'," he breathed.

"Good morning," she returned. "Coffee?"

"Sure." He set his niece down and followed Emily to the counter. "I wanted to get here early so you wouldn't have to look after Sophie."

She smiled at the child. "She wasn't a problem. We've been having fun."

Sophie nodded. "Yeah, we had fun. I'm gonna help

make breakfast, and after I come back from school, Emily said she will play dolls with me."

Reece realized how attached the child was getting to Emily. He needed to talk with Betty again about the sitter for Sophie. "You don't have to do this. There's got to be dozens of things you need to get finished before the crew gets here."

His eyes locked with hers as she handed him the mug. "There are, but until Jason needs me I think I can spend a little time with Sophie."

She raised her mug to her lips. Those soft, sweet lips that had him half crazy last night. So much that he hadn't thought about anything but his desire for her. And she was doing it to him again.

He took a sip of coffee, and realized, except for Sophie they were alone. "Where are Nate and Tori?"

"They're sleeping in. Nate said that when he gets up he wakes Tori. So he's staying in bed with his wife this morning."

Seeing the blush on Emily's cheeks, Reece figured the couple was doing more that just sleeping.

"So you get me for breakfast." Her blush deepened. "I mean, you'll have to settle for my cooking this morning."

"I'll help," Sophie said, refusing to be ignored.

He found himself smiling. "I know what you meant," Reece said to Emily. "And you don't need to cook anything for me."

He felt Sophie tug on his hand. "We want to cook for you, Unca Reece, 'cause you work so hard."

Sophie's big brown eyes stared up at him and his chest tightened. He glanced back at Emily. It was amazing the way she could act as if last night hadn't happened.

"Have you eaten?" she asked.

"No, but…"

"And neither have we." Emily went to the cupboard and pulled out plates. "Sophie, you set the table."

The girl happily took the dishes from her. Emily went to the refrigerator and removed a carton of eggs and some bacon.

Reece was right there to take the food from her. "You help Sophie and I'll cook for you ladies."

Emily held on. "You don't have to do that."

"You think I can't?" he asked, trying to make light of the situation, but when their gazes locked, he was lost.

"I didn't say that," she whispered in that soft voice of hers.

"Then sit down and I'll handle breakfast."

She stiffened. "Is that an order, Mr. McKellen?"

He'd never met anyone as stubborn as this woman. "It's a request, Ms. Hunter."

She stood her ground, raising her chin. "Then I like my eggs scrambled soft and my bacon crisp."

"Me, too," Sophie chimed.

Reece couldn't help but smile. He knew he was going to have his hands full with both ladies. But at this minute he didn't mind one bit.

At Jason's request later that morning, Reece and Emily rode out to the movie set. The hat Emily wore shielded her face from the sunlight, but nothing could diminish the sizzling Arizona heat. She'd been living in L.A. for the past few months where she'd been spoiled by the cool ocean breeze.

Finally they reached the clearing and the newly constructed cabin, barn and corral. They headed toward a stand of trees. Reece climbed off Toby and led his horse to the water trough to drink. Pulling off his gloves, he went to the spigot and primed the pump until cool spring water poured out.

Emily watched as Reece drank thirstily, then he removed his hat, bent lower and allowed the water to stream over his head. Her gaze lingered on his broad back and then slid down to his jeans. She admired the way the pants pulled taut over his tight butt. She sucked in a breath, feeling heated blood surging through her. *Man, oh man, am I in trouble.*

He suddenly turned to her. "You want some water?"

Oh, yes. She nodded and walked over. She cupped her hands and drank the water hoping that it would help cool her off. But one look at Reece with his hair slicked back and his damp T-shirt, and she knew she needed a deep freeze.

"I'm going to have a look inside the cabin," she said, backing up, but misjudged the step and started to fall backward. She gasped, but before she landed on the porch, Reece reached out and grabbed her by the arm.

"Whoa. You okay?" he asked.

"Yes, thank you," she breathed as she broke loose and hurried up the last step and into the cabin. The smell of newly cut wood assaulted her as she walked in. The large room consisted of rough logs that made up the walls, which were notched together to keep out the heat and the cold. The floor made of crudely split boards was partly covered by two braided rag rugs, one was in front of the huge stone fireplace, the other by the bunks built against one of the walls. There was an alcove where a double bed served as her great-great-grandparents' bedroom. Only the tie-back curtains added some privacy.

She walked over to the window in the kitchen area. It had been one of the few luxuries her ancestors had bought for their first home. Later, after their first few years on the Arizona plains, they'd purchased a maple table and the four chairs. Surprisingly Nate and Shane had found the furniture in the barn rafters during the ranch renovation. After refinishing the wood, it now provided the best seats in the cabin.

Emily smiled. Everything was as she'd pictured it. Just as her great-great-grandfather Jacob Hunter described in his journals.

The door opened and Reece walked in.

"Hey, it's not that hot in here," he said.

"Thank Shane," she told him. "He decided that it was just as easy to build in the shade as in the sun."

"I think the actors are going to be happy for that decision, too." He moved around the cabin. "This is nice."

"You really think so?" She found she cared about his opinion.

Reece could see that Emily wanted his approval. "I'd say a hundred years ago, this was first rate."

"My great-great-grandfather built the original cabin." She shook her head. "Jacob and Rebecca Hunter gave up a lot to settle here in Arizona."

"I'd say they made the right decision. Where did they come from?"

"Pennsylvania. Jacob's father wasn't the most upstanding citizen. Daniel Hunter was known as a schemer. He went after every get-rich-quick idea that came along. He gambled away the little money he made from working on the family farm.

"On the other side, my great-great-grandmother Rebecca was from society. The Palmers and Hunters were worlds apart, but one day Jacob and Rebecca met purely by chance. Young Jacob worked the farm, but also had a side job with an ice company in town. One day Jacob, who delivered for a company in town to make extra money, was making a delivery to the Palmer mansion and Rebecca was out in the garden. They met and from then on she made it a daily routine to visit with Jacob when he stopped by the Palmers's place to make his delivery. They'd talk about his dream of having his own ranch to raise cattle and horses. Needless to say, Rebecca's father didn't approve of his daughter's infatuation with a Hunter."

Emily smiled and Reece couldn't tell if he was intrigued more by her, or the story.

"I take it that didn't stop them," he said.

"Are you kidding? The Hunters are a stubborn bunch."

He was smiling now. "So you come by it honestly?"

Her back straightened. "I like to call it determination."

"Sure." He folded his arms as he leaned against the table. "Finish the story. Did Jacob sneak into Rebecca's room and steal her away?"

Emily shook her head. "No, Jacob planned to be noble. He was going to leave Rebecca to someone who could offer her more in life. She had plenty of suitors who could provide for her better than he could."

"So, he left for Arizona without her?" Reece asked.

"He tried. But Rebecca followed after him. She said she didn't care about material things. She only cared about hopes, dreams and loving someone so much that her life seemed senseless if she couldn't be with him."

Reece watched Emily blink back the tears in her eyes. "Right then and there, Jacob dropped to one knee and promised Rebecca all those things and asked her to be his wife. They were married that night, then boarded the train to Arizona. With what money they had, they bought a wagon, a team of horses and supplies. With the help of the Homestead Act they settled in a place Rebecca called a haven." She looked at Reece. "To learn the rest you're going to have to see the movie."

Reece reached over and jerked her braid. "Just how long have you been waiting to say that?"

She beamed and her eyes lit up. "A long time. Ever since my dad gave me Jacob's journal. And my dream is about to come true." He held her gaze for a long time. No matter how many times he told himself to back off, he couldn't deny the attraction, couldn't stop wanting to kiss her again.

Finally she looked away and stepped toward the door. "The heat's not going to go away so we better get a move on."

She was right about the heat. He was warm, but it had nothing to do with the Arizona sun.

By the time they'd made it back to the ranch, the place was buzzing with activity. More of the crew had arrived and were moving into the bunkhouse. Five trailers were lined up next to the barn and workers were busy checking to see if they were ready for their occupants.

At the barn, a ranch hand named Mike took Emily's and Reece's horses and told them about a meeting in the bunkhouse.

Jason met them at the door. "Good, you're back," he said. "Emily, I want you to meet Trent Justice."

The *Hunter's Haven*'s director wasn't much older than her brothers. He was about six feet tall with curly brown hair and warm hazel eyes. A pair of baggy, worn jeans and a plaid shirt covered his slight body.

"Emily, it's good to finally meet you," he told her as he offered her his hand. "I'm looking forward to getting started on this project."

She shook his hand as several people hovered in the background. "It's a pleasure to meet you, too."

Trent glanced over her shoulder. "Reece, it's good to see you again."

"Hi, Trent."

They knew each other? Emily wondered. How many movies had Reece worked on?

"How is the terrain around the set?" Trent asked.

"It's rough in a few spots, but nothing I can't avoid. If you don't need me anymore, I need see to the horses."

Trent nodded and walked Reece to the door. The two men spoke for a short time, then with a slap on the back from Trent, Reece left.

The director returned. "Sorry, I've worked with Reece on a few movies. You could say that we started out in this business together. I'm glad we got him on this project. He's the best."

Emily didn't doubt that. Not after she'd watched Reece's expert riding at the sight. He'd raced across the pasture as if he'd been flying. Of course he didn't have to be on horseback to get her attention.

Suddenly the screen door opened and a beautiful woman walked in.

"Jenny," Jason called as he went to the blue-eyed, blond actress and hugged her. He pulled back from the embrace. "You made it."

"I promised you I would." Her smile only enhanced her beauty. "I've been looking forward to doing this movie for months." She turned to the director. "And working again with you. Hi, Trent."

"Hi, Jen. I'm so glad our schedules were compatible." Trent led the actress to Emily. "Jennifer Tate, I'd like you to meet Emily Hunter. Emily, this is Jennifer."

"It's a pleasure, Emily, and please, call me Jenny."

"I'm honored that you accepted the role of Rebecca."

"Well, I'm going to do my best to live up to your wonderful story."

Jason stepped in. "Jenny, I'm sure that with you and Camden we're bound to be a success."

"That's only if I get top billing," a deep voice rang out as Camden Peters walked into the room. "Hello, Jennifer."

"Camden. Good to see you, too." The two stared at each other as sparks sizzled in the air between them. It was obvious that they knew each other. Suddenly Emily remembered reading a few years about how they'd been linked romantically.

"You always were a good liar, Jen."

"I guess it takes one to know one," the actress replied.

Trent stepped in. "Play nice, you two. We have a movie to make."

Emily felt a headache coming on.

Chapter Six

I've never worked so hard for anything in my en-
tire life. The days are an endless struggle just to
survive. Sometimes all I want to do is quit, but I
made a vow. Haven is our home now and we are
here to stay.
Jacob's Journal

The next week was a buzz of activity as the crew, the
gaffers and the movie grips arrived at the ranch. They
worked nonstop to get the generators and equipment set
up for the start of filming.

Emily didn't have much chance to stand around and
watch them. Her days were spent at a temporary desk in
either her old bedroom, or at the bunkhouse kitchen table rewriting sections of the opening scene. Trent had sug-

gested changes and Camden had ideas to beef up his part. It wasn't that she minded, but she hated the isolation.

She had gotten to know the crew when they came in for meals, or when she'd attended some of Jenny and Camden's readings. Jason promised her that she'd be front and center when they filmed the first scene.

Reece had been kept busy, too. He worked with Toby and Camden going over the different stunt scenes. And since Jennifer Tate would be riding Shadow, he'd been spending time with her, too.

The gorgeous actress was a good horsewoman, so why did she need Reece's supervision? Emily chided herself for writing so many adventurous episodes into the script. And for even caring what Reece McKellen did or who he did it with.

After finishing the rewrites on the opening scene, Emily handed them over to Trent and decided to head to town. She needed to get away, to have a night to relax and sleep. She wasn't due back at the ranch until late the next day, so she could sleep in.

Twenty minutes later she pulled into her mother's driveway, but her enthusiasm quickly died when she saw that the house was dark. Her mother had gone out, probably with Sam. It seemed that everyone in her family had someone except her.

She glanced toward the garage and saw a light on in the apartment above. A smile curved her lips as she thought about Sophie. Now that the girl was in school all morning and spent the afternoons with her teenage sitter, she hadn't had much of a chance to visit with the child. Emily was amazed how attached she'd gotten to the little girl and her uncle.

It irritated her to admit it, but she'd missed Reece, too. Had he missed her? Had he thought about the kiss they'd shared? Stop it, she scolded herself. There was no need for her to be thinking about a man right now. The last thing Emily needed was to start up a romance.

Emily headed for her mother's back door when she saw Reece and Sophie come out of the apartment.

Telling herself she just wanted to say a quick hello to Sophie, Emily waited as the child and her uncle descended the steps.

"Emily!" the little girl cried, running toward her.

Emily bent down and hugged her. Who would have thought those tiny arms could feel so good? "I've missed you, Sophie," she whispered and pulled back. "I hear you like school."

Sophie's dark eyes widened. "It's fun. I get to color, and Tori helps me with my words and numbers, so I can go to kindergarten next year." Her expression changed. "But I miss you and Unca Reece."

I miss him too, Emily thought. "Well, maybe one day soon you can spend a day at the ranch. Once the movie gets going." She glanced up to where Reece was standing just a few feet away. "Hi," she said.

"Hi."

He looked good, but then, he always looked good. His hair was damp and his face cleanly shaven. He wore clean jeans and a black T-shirt.

"Well, I won't keep you," she hedged as she stood.

"I'll go visit with my mother and let you two get back to your evening."

"Unca Reece and me are going on a date," Sophie said. "Want to go with us?"

Talk about an awkward moment. "Oh, Sophie, that's very nice of you to ask, but I think this is a special night for you and your uncle."

"But I want you to go, too. Please." The child glanced up at her uncle. "Can Emily come?"

Reece looked at her. "It's fine with me. We're just going to the café."

"For hamburgers," Sophie added. "So you need to come."

Emily raised an eyebrow at Reece.

He shrugged. "I told Sophie it's her night and her choice. If she wants you to come along, then please do."

Emily smiled. "That's a hard invitation to turn down."

Reece had been surprised to see Emily in town. All week he'd been telling himself it was for the best that she hadn't been around to distract him. But, she didn't even have to be there to sneak into his thoughts.

"Then let's go." The huskiness of his voice surprised him. "Sophie has missed you." *And, so have I….*

They walked through the café doors to find a small supper crowd and soft music playing on the jukebox. Sophie picked out a booth and insisted on sitting beside Emily.

"You sit over there, Unca Reece." Sophie told him happily, pointing to the other side of the booth just as they were greeted by the middle-aged waitress, Margaret.

"Well, who do we have here?" Margaret said as she set glasses filled with water before each of them.

"We're on a date," Sophie told her.

Reece watched as Emily's cheeks reddened. "Hi, Margaret," she said. "This is Reece McKellen and Sophie, his niece. Reece is the stuntman on the movie."

"My unca Reece does tricks on his horse."

"Well, isn't that exciting," the waitress said.

"Is Sam here tonight?" Emily asked.

"No, he took the night off. Ben is at the grill."

"Maybe we should order," Reece said. "Emily."

"The dinner special with iced tea."

"I'll have the same," Reece said, then turned to Sophie. "And for my date…"

Sophie glanced over the menu. "I want a hamburger and apple sauce and chocolate ice cream."

"And a glass of milk," Reece said.

Sophie placed her hands over her mouth an giggled. "This is fun."

"Best date I've ever been on," Reece assured her. And you chose a good place to come and eat." He turned to Emily. "What about you, are you having fun?"

"I always have fun here. The Good Time Café is the best place in town to bring a date."

Sophie's eyes rounded. "Really?"

Emily nodded. "All the high school kids come here."

"Did Tori and Mariah?"

"Well, Mariah and Shane hung out when they were

teenagers. But Tori came from San Francisco, but before she married Nate, she used to work here. Back then if you wanted Sheriff Nate you would find him seated at the counter."

"And they fell in love," the child said. "And they got married and got a baby."

"Yeah, that's how it happened," Emily agreed.

Reece smiled and her heart tripped. "I guess you could say the café has a reputation for bringing people together."

He was flirting with her. "Since it was the only place in town to hang out and dance. Yeah, everyone likes coming here."

Suddenly the music stopped and the room grew quiet.

"Hey, Sophie," Emily said. "If you can get a quarter from your uncle, we'll go to the jukebox and play some music."

As on cue, Sophie smiled. "Please, Unca Reece, can I have a quarter."

Reece raised an eyebrow. "She never used to ask for money before she started hanging out with you," he said and he dug coins from his pocket.

Emily stood with a smile. "Get used to it, cowboy, it's only the beginning." Taking Sophie's hand they headed to the jukebox.

Reece couldn't help but notice the gentle sway of her hips and her long slender legs. He blew out a long breath. He was going to get into trouble if he kept thinking about this woman.

It only got worse when the familiar song, "My Girl," began. As the other patrons watched, Emily began to dance with Sophie. He couldn't help smiling at her carefree way with the child. She was so good with his niece. He could see that she honestly cared for Sophie.

Sophie ran to him and tugged on his arm. "You have to dance, too," she insisted.

"Okay," he said, reluctantly climbing to his feet and made his way to the dance floor and Emily. The music changed to a Righteous Brothers ballad, "Unchained Melody." He swung his niece up into his arms and began to sway to the music.

She giggled. "Wait, Emily has to dance with us." She waved for her.

When Emily stepped closer, the child gave directions. "Now put your arm on Unca Reece's shoulders." By the time, Sophie finished, they were in an intimate circle. Reece could smell the lemony scent of Emily's hair, and when she turned to look at him, he was quickly mesmerized by her eyes.

"This is fun," Sophie said.

Reece was thinking of a different description of having Emily so close. It was somewhere between pleasure and pain.

"She's finally asleep," Reece said as he came out of the bedroom. "She put up a fight and went down only after I'd agreed to read her another bedtime story."

Emily smiled, knowing it was time for her to leave.

PLAY THE
Lucky Key Game

and you can get

Do You Have the LUCKY KEY?

FREE BOOKS
and a FREE GIFT!

Scratch the gold areas with a coin. Then check below to see the books and gift you can get!

YES!

I have scratched off the gold areas. Please send me the 2 FREE BOOKS and GIFT for which I qualify. I understand I am under no obligation to purchase any books, as explained on the back of this card.

310 SDL D7YZ   210 SDL D7YF

FIRST NAME   LAST NAME

ADDRESS

APT.#   CITY

STATE/PROV.   ZIP/POSTAL CODE

2 free books plus a free gift   1 free book

2 free books   Try Again!

www.eHarlequin.com

If offer card is missing write to: Silhouette Reader Service, 3010 Walden Ave., P.O. Box 1867, Buffalo NY 14240-1867

BUSINESS REPLY MAIL
FIRST-CLASS MAIL   PERMIT NO. 717-003   BUFFALO, NY

POSTAGE WILL BE PAID BY ADDRESSEE

SILHOUETTE READER SERVICE
3010 WALDEN AVE
PO BOX 1867
BUFFALO NY 14240-9952

NO POSTAGE
NECESSARY
IF MAILED
IN THE
UNITED STATES

She needed a good night's sleep, too. Besides, Reece had only invited her along because Sophie had insisted on her joining them. An ache began in her chest and settled in her stomach. Tonight had been a bad idea. She was getting too attached to this child. Emily knew that when it was time for Reece and Sophie to leave, she would be hurt.

"Well, thank you for letting me intrude on your date." She started for the door.

"It's still early. What do you say to a cup of coffee?"

Tell him no and just leave, she ordered herself. "I'm not sure I should."

He looked at her with those sexy dark eyes. "I need a favor."

"Sure." Her heart was pounding in her chest as he filled two mugs and brought them to the coffee table.

"I added milk and one sugar," he told her. "That's how you take it, isn't it?"

With a nod, she sank onto the sofa and cradled the warm cup in her hands.

He sat down next to her. "Does the offer still stand about taking Sophie shopping? I know you're busy now, but Sophie really needs some things."

She was surprised. "No problem," she said. "What does she need?"

"Well, as you know, her wardrobe is pretty limited. And since Sophie's been in school, she's been voicing an opinion on what she wants." His gaze settled on Emily once again. "Six weeks ago, I could barely get her to say a word. Now, as you've seen, she's become quite a chatterbox." He shook his head as a smile creased his mouth. "She reminds me a lot of Carrie."

Emily could also see a flash of sadness on his eyes. "You miss your sister, don't you?"

He shrugged. "I hadn't seen her in years, but she was pretty stubborn when she was Sophie's age." He glanced away as if to say he wasn't ready to talk about his past. "I know you're busy, but I'd appreciate any help."

"Sure. I'm not expected at the ranch until the afternoon tomorrow. Why don't you make a list of things Sophie needs and I'll take her shopping in the morning and then bring her out to the ranch after we're finished."

"I have to be out at the ranch by seven. I'm doing a run-through on one of the scenes with Jenny Tate, but I should be free in the afternoon to take Sophie," he said.

Emily tried not to react to the fact that Reece was going to spend time with the beautiful actress. "I watched Jenny the other day. She rides very well."

"She's doing all her own riding, but we still have to choreograph it."

Of course they did. Why wasn't she thinking logically? But was she supposed to believe that Reece hadn't noticed that Jennifer Tate was drop-dead gorgeous? Not her business. "Have you ever gotten hurt on a stunt?"

Reece leaned back on the sofa. "Not badly. Not like in my rodeo days. That's one of the reasons I went into stuntwork."

"Then why are you leaving? Is it because of Sophie?"

He shook his head. "She's only made my plans to retire more immediate. I've been wanting out for a while now." He sighed. "I've gotten tired of the whole Hollywood scene."

"You're talking about people like…Camden?"

"I'm not crazy about how he uses his stardom or women. Is he treating you okay?"

"He's been fine. And why would he be interested in me when Jennifer Tate is around?"

He looked at her, his gaze heated and searching. "Why wouldn't he go after a beautiful woman?"

How was she supposed to react to a comment like that? "Well, you don't have to worry about me, I've managed to take care of myself for years. And I can recognize a man's line when I hear it. But thanks for the advice." She stood. "Just drop Sophie off at the house in the morning."

Reece got up and followed her to the door. "Look, Emily, I didn't mean…"

She swung around and waited for him to finish.

"Thanks for coming tonight. Sophie had a good time…and so did I."

She smiled. "I had fun, too. Thanks for inviting me. Good night, Reece." Not wanting to prolong the awkward tension between them, Emily hurried out the door and on to the dark porch just in time to see two silhouettes standing inside the kitchen doorway below. Good, her mother and Sam were home.

She was about to go down the steps when the two figures slowly blended into one. Emily froze as Sam held her mother in his arms and kissed her. The kiss wasn't a friendly peck and it wasn't on the cheek.

Their kiss wasn't one between friends. It was a kiss shared by lovers.

Suddenly Emily felt Reece's hand on her arm as he tugged her back into the apartment.

"Was your mother expecting you home tonight?"

Emily only shook her head, remembering she'd parked behind the garage so her car wasn't visible from the house.

She blew out a breath. "I just never realized... I mean I knew they cared about each other. But I figured they were older and..."

"Couldn't be hot for each other," Reece finished.

"That's not the way I pictured my mother, or Sam," she said.

"I saw it right away. Every time Sam looked at your mother. The man's crazy about her."

Emily had seen it, too. There'd been a tenderness and caring, but not the heated passion that she had just witnessed between them. "It's just seeing your mother kiss someone like that..." She couldn't be jealous that her mother had someone, could she? "I love Sam. He's always been like a member of the family."

"He seems like a nice guy." Reece's gaze pinned her to the door. "What are you going to do?"

"Well, I'm not going to go down there and disturb them. Is it okay if I wait here?" She inhaled. "Oh, no, what if he stays the night?"

"He doesn't, as a rule," Reece told her.

She raised her hand as a heated blush crept over her face. "Please! I don't want to know anymore."

Reece glanced over her shoulder. "Looks like your mother went into the house, and Sam is heading to his truck."

Even as Emily tried to keep their relationship all business, she realized she was drawn to this man. Standing so close to Reece, she could smell a hint of his aftershave. Intoxicating.

"I think he's gone," he said in a husky voice.

She blinked. "Oh, then I should go."

"That's probably best," he told her. "It's late." In the shadows, she could see as he lowered head.

"I know." Lord help her, she couldn't stop him.

"This is a bad idea," he warned her. "But you're just too damn distracting."

Reece cupped for face, leaned down and kissed her. His mouth was warm and inviting, immediately coaxing a response from her. Her arms moved up his chest, feeling his rapid heart beat. He caught her lower lip between his teeth and tugged gently, then drew back, his dark gaze searching hers.

Emily wanted nothing more than to get lost in his arms, in his kiss, but she couldn't. "I think this is a distraction neither of us needs right now." She pushed him away and walked out the door.

Two days later, Emily sat beside Jason and watched Trent direct the actors to their marks. Although the opening scene of the movie would be filmed in a studio in L.A., today was the first day of filming at the ranch. And finally a chance for Emily to slow down since she left Reece's apartment.

The morning after, she'd been too busy with Sophie to have time to talk to her mother about Sam. Not that she knew what to say. Actually it really wasn't any of her business. So instead of the dreaded conversation with her mother, she took Sophie shopping. They'd had a lot of fun picking out jeans and Western blouses. With colder weather coming, she'd made sure that Sophie also had a coat and sweaters.

By the time they'd arrived at the ranch, Emily found it hard to give Sophie up. Yet, the minute she saw her uncle, she took off running. Emily found she wanted to run to Reece, too, for a repeat of the prior night's kiss. Instead she'd left them and went to finish her rewrites.

"Quiet!" the director's assistant called, bringing Emily back to the present. A hush came over the crew and everyone prepared to do their jobs. The cameras were positioned to face the valley.

Emily's heart pounded with excitement as she gazed toward the open field and four horses harnessed to a wagon. Jennifer and Camden sat on the seat waiting for their cue.

"*Hunter's Haven,* scene one, take one," the assistant announced.

"And action," Trent called and motioned for Camden and Jenny, representing Jacob and Rebecca Hunter, to begin.

Jacob slapped the reins against the horses' rumps. The team plodded off, causing the couple to bounce on the wooden seat of the loaded wagon. The journey across the open field was rough and they finally came to a stop by the creek.

Jacob climbed down and reached back to assist his bride. Once they were on the ground she laughed as he swung her around.

"It's all ours, Becky. All one hundred and sixty-five acres. Later, we will have more." He grinned. "It's Hunter land."

"Oh, Jacob." There were tears in her eyes. "It's beautiful here." She looked toward the brown and orange hues of the mountain range, back again across the high grassy field, to the cool water of the creek.

Her husband took her in his arms. "We can make a good life here. And I'll prove your father wrong."

"Oh, Jacob, you don't have to prove anything to my father, or me."

"Maybe not," he breathed. "But I need to prove something to myself." His intense blue eyes locked with his bride's. "This is a new start. No more carrying the shame of being Joe Hunter's son." He rested his hands on his hips. "Mark this date, Becky, June 6, 1904. From this day, I'm going to make the name Hunter mean something important here.

Here I have that chance with you," he said determinedly as he pulled her into his arms. "Your love makes me believe I can do anything."

Tears welled up in her eyes. "Oh, Jacob, you can do

anything. Look how you've followed your dream to this special place. You're going to build a wonderful life here."

He smiled. "And I've already started. This morning while you were packing at the hotel, I purchased a breeding bull and small herd of Herefords. They'll be delivered in a few days."

Becky gasped. "But, Jacob, we haven't even built a place to live."

He raised a hand. "We will. I've already met two of our neighbors at the stockyards. We're going to help each other. The barn has to come first. That means we'll have to sleep in the wagon for the next few weeks." Concern furrowed his brow. "Becky, I know you're not used to this kind of life, but—"

"Stop it, Jacob. You are my husband. I will always stay by your side," she said and smiled. "It will be an adventure to sleep under the beautiful Arizona sky. And just think what an adventure we'll have to tell our children about years from now."

His eyes focused on hers. "Oh, Becky, I want to give you the world."

"I don't need the world. I have your love, and now, this haven. What else could I want?" She reached up and pressed her mouth to his. Jacob took his wife in his arms and deepened the kiss.

"And...cut," the director called as the actors slowly broke off the kiss, then stepped back from each other.

"That was great," Trent said.

Embarrassed, Emily wiped the tears off her check.

She'd never realized how emotional it would be to watch Jacob and Becky's story come to life.

"You okay?"

Emily turned around to find Reece standing behind her chair. "I'm fine." She stood and walked away from the crew and their activities. Once shielded by an old oak tree, she leaned against the trunk, and tried to pull herself together.

Reece followed her. "I have to say one thing, Camden is doing a good job," he admitted.

"Yes, he is. And so is Jenny. They made me forget that they were acting. It all seemed so real. They not only spoke my words, but showed my great-great-grandfather's feelings for his bride." Tears clogged in her throat.

Reece tipped his cowboy hat back. "This is your family history, Emily. You have a right to be proud and emotional."

"Oh, I am proud, Reece. I just didn't expect to feel so moved just… seeing Camden and Jenny playing Jacob and Becky." She touched her heart. "It got to me."

"Sometimes feelings have a way of sneaking up on you. Suddenly you're blindsided by them and there isn't a damn thing to do about it."

Emily's gaze went to his mouth and she couldn't help but think about their kiss the other night. Her entire body still tingled from wanting him.

"You better stop looking at me like that."

"Like how?" she asked innocently, thrilled that he, too, was fighting the attraction between them.

Reece leaned in closer and she could see the golden flecks in his eyes. "Just understand, I have a job to do and that's all."

Emily's heart pounded as he took a step closer. "I can't afford to get lost in you, Em," he whispered. "We're both headed in different directions."

Chapter Seven

Today is one of the happiest days of my life. Becky told me she's expecting our first child in late spring. I am joyous, but I'm concerned for her. Life is hard here, but Becky insists that she's strong enough to handle it.
Jacob's Journal

The next Friday evening, Emily was sitting in Jennifer Tate's trailer.

"Come on, Emily, you can't change your mind," the actress coaxed as she looped her belt through her tight-fitting jeans. "You have to go with us. We need to celebrate the end of a successful week of filming. And we have tomorrow off to sleep in."

"But I still have to rework Monday's scene."

Jenny frowned. "You can take off a few hours for some fun." The pretty blonde checked her lipstick in the trailer mirror.

Emily's heart wasn't into partying. Although they'd been on schedule, it had been a difficult week. She'd been stuck inside rewriting scenes most of the time. She'd even missed Reece's first stunt. Not that she should care, but she did. She did get to see the film footage, and that had been all she'd seen of the man since the first day of shooting. Of course, Emily hadn't seen much of anyone other than Trent and Jason.

Jenny's voice broke into her thoughts. "I bet there's a lot of good-looking cowboys who'd be happy to kick up their heels. It's been so long since I've gone dancing."

Emily thought back to last week. Her so-called date. Technically she guessed what she'd done with Reece and Sophie could be considered dancing. A warm shiver slid down her body recalling his hand around her waist. She could almost feel the way his dark eyes had pierced her, causing her to forget to breathe, and later how his kiss had nearly consumed her.

"Emily?"

Hearing her name called, she shook away the thought. "What?"

Jenny frowned. "That settles it, you've been working way too hard. You're going on a girls' night out. Kim, Heather and Sally are coming, too, and since you know your way around, we need you tell us where to go."

She caved in. "Well that all depends on whether you want quiet and subdued, or adventurous and a little wild."

Jenny smiled as she grabbed her purse and tugged Emily toward the door. "Definitely wild."

"Then it's the Wild Mustang Bar."

Thirty minutes later, their white van pulled off the highway into the gravel parking lot of the bar. Emily knew her brothers would kill her if they knew she was there. It was a good thing they would never find out. She could hear the sound of country and western music even before they walked through the swinging bar doors.

Several heads turned as Jenny walked inside. Emily smiled. She didn't mind the actress getting the attention. How many people got to spend an evening with Jennifer Tate? By the looks of the cowboys three-deep at the bar, there were plenty of men to go around. And Emily was determined to find herself one, or maybe two. She wasn't going to think about Reece McKellen. No way. Tonight, she was going to flirt and share a few dances with some good-looking strangers.

At the bar, Reece raised the longneck bottle to his lips and took a deep swallow. How had he let the guys talk him into coming here? This place reminded him too much of his rodeo days.

His thoughts turned to his new charge, Sophie. Things had changed since she'd come into his life. She seemed happy even despite the fact he'd been stumbling along playing daddy. Her new independence surprised him, too. He checked his watch.

Sophie was at the movies with Betty and Sam, then she was going to spend the night with Betty. He couldn't face the empty apartment so he ended up here.

Suddenly he caught sight of a familiar, tall brunette. He walked toward the dance floor to get a better look and sure enough Emily was two-stepping with some cowboy. His chest tightened. He didn't like the man's familiarity. What the hell should he care? He marched back to the bar and ordered another beer.

Emily was tired. Mainly she was tired of this guy's hands all over her. Finally she told him she wanted to find her friends. She walked off the dance floor and looked around for Jenny. Instead, she found Reece McKellen.

"Just what I don't need," she murmured. The music changed as another cowboy came up to her. But before he could ask her to dance, she felt Reece's hand on her arm, pulling her away.

Emily wanted to stop him, but when he drew her into his arms, she lost her voice as he expertly led her around the dance floor. Then the music changed to Garth Brooks's song "Shameless." Reece's steps slowed and his hold tightened as he pulled her closer. Emily shivered as her breasts brushed against his chest, she felt an erotic friction as her thighs rubbed against his.

He finally spoke. "What are you doing in a place like this?"

"Same thing you are. Trying to have a good time. Where's Sophie?"

"She's with your mother and Sam."

"So it looks like we're both out to have a little fun."

"That guy you were dancing with wants more than a little two-steppin'."

She blinked at his protectiveness. "I can handle him."

He made a snorting sound. "You don't belong in a place like this."

"Look, I can take care of myself. Besides, most of these guys know I'm the sheriff's sister. Believe me, they aren't going to try anything."

"You don't exactly bring out the common sense in a man."

Before Emily could respond a commotion drew their attention across the room where Jenny was arguing with some guy. Reece hurried to her aid and Emily was right behind him. But Camden Peters reached Jenny first and drew her out of harm's way.

It was Reece who held the drunk back. "She was dancing with me," the man slurred. "Get your own girl."

"One dance isn't a commitment," Jenny announced.

"Honey, that's because you haven't given me a chance to work my charm."

That drew laughter from the crowd and a smile from Jenny. "Sorry, cowboy, you're going to have to save it."

"Just give me one more dance."

Camden stepped in. "Come on, cowboy. You already had too much to drink."

"What business is it of yours?"

Camden's gaze went to Jenny. "I'm hoping a lot more than yours?"

Just then the bouncer showed up and took the drunk outside.

The other patrons began to boo. But Camden grew their attention. "Look, we're here for a good time like everyone else. So how about a round of drinks for everyone?"

"Well, I guess men are the same everywhere," Jenny said, watching as the actor walked to the bar with several new friends in tow.

"You want to leave?" Emily asked.

"No." She beamed at Reece. "At least not until I have a dance with this cowboy." Jenny tugged Reece out onto the dance floor.

Emily just stood there. She didn't want to feel jealous, but dammit, she did. What did she expect? Reece wasn't hers. Just because he had danced with her. And they shared a few kisses....

Wasn't that what she wanted? No strings. She glanced at the couple on the floor. They were laughing. Why did Reece have to show up tonight? Why did he have to be the one who stirred her heart?

She shook away the thought. What was wrong with her? She had a movie to worry about.

"Hi, beautiful. You're looking mighty lonely."

She glanced over her shoulder. "Oh, Camden. I didn't see you."

The handsome actor frowned. "I'm crushed. I guess I'll have to find a way to get your attention." A slow song began. "We have to work on that. I believe this is our dance."

He led her to the floor, then pulled her close and easily picked up the rhythm. "I never give up a chance to hold a beautiful woman in my arms."

Camden Peters was a handsome man. Any woman would die for his attention, but she couldn't share his enthusiasm. Emily glanced in Reece's direction.

Unfortunately her heart was in danger of being captured by a man who was obviously having a good time with another woman.

Four days later, Reece pulled the strap through the ring on Shadow's cinch and tugged it tight. Satisfied that the horse was ready, he took the mare by the reins and led her toward Jenny.

"Thanks, Reece," Jenny said. She was dressed as Becky for the next scene in a pair of men's trousers and an oversize shirt. The hat on her head was a little big, emphasizing her small frame.

"Just let Shadow do her job," Reece instructed as he rubbed the horse's neck. "She won't let you down."

After Jenny nodded, Reece helped her mount the horse. She rode across the field to where cameras were set up.

Reece went back to Toby and climbed on. He was dressed in the same period wardrobe as Camden. He pushed his hat down on his head as the director motioned for Jenny to start her ride.

He watched as she rode down the road. Excitement

radiated across her smiling face. Finally she spotted the herd and Camden. She called out "Jacob" and kicked the horse's sides to pick up some speed. Once off the road, she was meant to suddenly encounter a snake. On command, Shadow whinnied and reared up. Jenny screamed as the horse took off in a gallop.

"Perfect," Reece whispered, then kicked Toby and the horse shot off after the runaway. Sensing the camera on him, he kept his head down until rode up beside Shadow. He leaned over, reached around Jenny's waist and pulled her off the horse onto his lap. She placed her arms around his neck.

Once Toby came to a stop, he heard the director call cut. Jenny looked up at him and smiled. "My hero."

He gave a sharp whistle to Shadow. "Careful, Jenny, you'll give me a big head."

"I don't mind," she said. "As long as you don't drop me."

Camden put in an appearance. "Okay, McKellen, your job is done. My turn."

Reece wasn't going to let Peters get to him. "If you think you can handle it." He helped Jenny down first, then swung off Toby.

The director arrived. "That was great, you two. I'm sure we got everything in one take."

Reece strode off to retrieve Shadow and rewarded her with an apple. That was when he spotted Emily. Dressed in her jeans, boots and Western blouse, she definitely didn't look like she belonged in L.A. He was also surprised how hungry he'd been just for the sight of her all week. He hadn't been able to stop thinking about their being together. But she'd been keeping her distance.

Emily said something to Camden that made them both smile. Reece tensed. Fine. Why should he care? She could spend time with anyone she wanted.

She walked over to him. "Great scene." She rubbed Shadow's neck. "And you, girl, are really the star. What a performance."

"Jenny did some of the work." Reece glanced at her. "You're lucky she knows how to ride."

Emily didn't need to hear any more accolades for Jenny. So she was beautiful. She could act and even ride a horse. And Emily had to admit that she was a nice person. "She's doing a great job playing Becky."

Reece wasn't even listening to her. He was busy watching Camden in the saddle with Jenny seated in his lap.

The director's assistant called for quiet and the area went silent. "And action."

"You foolhardy woman," Jacob said as he cuddled his wife close. "What possessed you…?"

"I've been riding since I was five, Jacob Hunter. I know how to handle a horse."

He shook his head. "All I can think about is what could have happened." He pulled back to look her in the eyes. "I don't know what I would do without you." The emotions made his voice husky.

"Jacob, I'm fine. And I'm not going anywhere. I was just anxious to see you," she said as tears filled her eyes. "It's been over a week since you've been home."

With a jerk of the reins, Jacob turned the horse and began walking back toward the road. "Becky, you know that I have to stay with the herd."

"I understand that, and I just couldn't wait for you get back. I wanted to come out and share my news."

"It can't be so important that it couldn't wait until I returned—"

"I'm going to have a baby," she whispered. "We're going to have a baby."

Jacob's eyes widened, then filled with tenderness. "A baby? It's only been a few months... Are you sure?"

She nodded. "Emma Summers took me to see the doctor. He said the baby should be here in the spring."

"Oh, Becky, I love you so much." He touched her cheek. "We're really going to be a family."

"Yes, we are. So you better finish the cabin. I don't want our baby living in the barn."

"Anything you want."

She put her arms around his neck. "This baby is a bonus, because I have everything I want. You."

Jacob Hunter lowered his mouth to hers and kissed her.

It was after seven o'clock Friday night and Emily was exhausted, glad another week of filming was over. She pulled her car into her mother's driveway. This time she'd called ahead to ask if she had any plans.

Betty Hunter told her she only wanted to spend a quiet evening with her daughter. That was what Emily wanted, too. Making this movie had been a lot more draining than she'd anticipated and though she didn't want to admit it, "all-business relationship" with Reece McKellen had her in knots. If only she could stay away from Reece nothing would happen. So that had been what she'd done all week. Unfortunately it wasn't working.

She shook her head and got out of the car. Somehow she needed to find a way to stay away from him. The man could break her heart. She passed the steps leading to the garage apartment. *Just keep walking and don't look up, she warned herself. Go talk to your mother.*

Emily made it to the back door when she heard the sounds of a child crying. Was Sophie in trouble? Was the little girl hurt?

She turned around and listened. She heard another heart wrenching sob that Emily couldn't ignore. It was definitely Sophie. She went up the steps and knocked on the door. Finally Reece answered.

He looked panicked. "I don't know what to do."

Emily entered and found the little girl curled up on the sofa. "Sophie." She touched the child. "What's wrong? Do you hurt somewhere?"

Emily was relieved when Sophie shook her head. "No."

"Can you tell your uncle Reece or me what's wrong?"

"I want my mommy."

Emily's heart flooded with sympathy. She sat down next to the child and took her into her arms. "Oh, baby, I'm so sorry you're sad. You know your mother went to heaven."

Sophie rubbed her eyes. "But I don't want her in heaven. I want her to be here. All my friends at school have a mommy. All but me. I wish…"

Tears welled up in Emily's eyes and the familiar pain of her own father's death filled her. At any age, the loss of a parent was devastating.

"We can wish for lots of things, Sophie, but sometimes they aren't possible." Emily glanced at Reece, recognizing the torment on his face.

"Remember the other day when I told you my daddy died?" She felt the child's head nod. "I was so sad for a long time. All my friends still had their daddies. Then Sam told me that my daddy loved me so much he would never want me to be sad. That I should always remember special things about him and keep them in my heart, so when I got sad, I could pull out those memories and I'd be happy again."

She cupped Sophie's chin and made the child look at her. "You want to try to remember some happy times?"

The girl swiped her tears and nodded. "'Kay."

"I'll start," Emily said. "I remember that my dad built me a tree swing when I was little. And he used to push me so high that my stomach tickled. And I thought I could touch the sky." She smiled and looked at the child. "Your turn."

Sophie sat up as her tiny hands brushed the hair out of her face. "My mommy used to take me to the park." She used to hold me up so I could grab hold of the monkey bars and she promised she'd never let me go."

"What else?" Emily coaxed.

"Sometimes we had a tickle fight. And she used to read me a story every night and rub my back so I'd go to sleep. I had to be real quiet so Jerry wouldn't get mad. He didn't like kids."

Reece knelt down beside the two. "Well, I like kids," he said. "Especially little girls with curly hair and big brown eyes. And I will always be here for you." He hugged her as his gaze met Emily's. Her heart melted.

The child pulled away. "Do you like Emily, too?"

His eyes locked with Emily's, his gaze intent. "Yes, I like Emily, too."

The tremor in his voice caused Emily to shiver.

"Can she stay and read me a story?"

"Sure, but you need to be ready for bed first, and only one story. It's late."

The child scrambled off, leaving the two adults alone.

Reece stood up and rubbed his hands over his face. "Thanks for saving me," he told her. "I didn't know what to do."

"She's going to have problems again. I know how hard it was on me, and I was a lot older."

He started to reach a hand to touch her, then suddenly pulled back. "Sometimes this parenting thing gets so overwhelming."

"Not that I'm experienced in that department, but I do know it's very important that you spend time with Sophie."

"How can I? I can't stop my work on the movie?"

"You don't need to be with her 24/7, but more than you have been. Let her go to school, but have Tori bring her back to the ranch in the afternoons. She needs to know that you aren't going to desert her. And when you can't be with her, then one of us will be, or the sitter. But let her be close by."

"I can't ask you to do that."

"You're not asking. I'm offering. I know my mother would gladly help out. If you haven't noticed, she's very fond of Sophie."

"And Sophie is coming to care for your family. What's going to happen when we have to leave here?"

My heart's going to break, Emily cried silently. "We'll stay in touch. That's what friends do."

He stood there for a long time and studied her. He finally took a step closer. "Is that what you want us to be, Emily? Friends?"

Her chest tightened and she started to reach out to him just as Sophie called out her name.

"Coming," Emily called back and looked at Reece. "Yes, I'd like us to be friends." She smiled, then took off down the hall, before she confessed she wished they could be much, much more.

Chapter Eight

Many of homesteader had called it quits. Some returned home, others went to work in the silver mines to feed their families. It's hard to tell our friends goodbye, knowing we'll never see some of them again.
Jacob's Journal

After two weeks Emily had come to the conclusion that filming a movie wasn't as glamorous as she'd once thought. It was hard work.

Today was no exception.

The sizzling July sun had made everyone eager to finish, especially after several retakes of one scene. Soon the actors' and crew's patience grew thin and tempers erupted.

Finally Trent halted the day's shooting, but called the cast members to a meeting at the bunkhouse. Everyone else had been dismissed until seven in the morning. Emily didn't have to be told twice and climbed into the air-conditioned van for the ride back to the ranch house.

As she had several times in the past fourteen days, she searched for Reece. As usual he was busy tending to the animals. He and another wrangler were rounding up the cattle to pen them up for the night.

A natural on a horse, Reece sat in the saddle as if he was born to it. An easy hand held the reins as he moved as one with his mount. Oh, he was a pleasure to watch. Toby was an expert cutting horse, catching up to every steer, then directing them toward the pen. She could easily picture both the man and the horse on a ranch.

Emily closed her eyes. *The man's not for you,* she chanted to herself just as she had since that night in his apartment. If only she could erase the memory of his kisses from her head, and banish the feelings he caused whenever he got close.

Not that he'd been near her lately. Reece had done everything to avoid her. After he'd finished shooting for the day, he'd pick up Sophie and head back to town. He couldn't have made it any clearer that he didn't want her in his life.

The van bounced over the rough dirt road and tears formed in her eyes. What had happened to her? She'd planned to be the successful career woman. She was going to take Hollywood by storm. There was no room in her life for a man, least of all a man with a child. The image of Sophie with her big brown eyes, and those sweet little hands reaching out to her made her heart ache.

Reece McKellen wasn't hard on the eyes, either. All he had to do was give her one of his heated looks and she was lost. And his kisses… Emily quickly pushed away that thought.

She had to resign herself to the fact that all they ever could be was friends. And after this project, Reece and Sophie would leave Haven for good.

The van pulled in behind the barn. Emily climbed out, but was too antsy to go up to the house. Maybe a few hours alone would help. She went into the barn just as Nate came out of his workshop.

"Hey, you're back early," he said.

"Too hot. You're finished for the day, too."

"Yeah. I just couldn't get into carving today. Tori hasn't been feeling well."

Emily smiled. "Well, the big day is approaching fast."

He nodded and exhaled. "Two weeks."

"She's not watching Sophie, is she?"

"No. Mom took her over to the café." He smiled. "Sophie said 'Sam's gonna teach me to dance the old way.'"

Her mother and Sam. How many times over the years had the two spent time together, and Emily had never realized they had feelings for each other? "Nate…have you ever thought about Mom and Sam…as a couple?"

Nate smiled. "Yeah. Why?"

She didn't know if she should bring it up. "It's just

the other night... I saw... I mean... I didn't tell Mom I was coming home and I saw her and Sam kissing."

Nate's smile turned into a big grin. "Well, I'll be damned. So he's finally making a move."

"What do you mean?"

"Come on, Em. Sam's been crazy about Mom for years. I think he thought she could never have feelings for anyone else but Dad. So he's stayed in the background." Her brother shook his head. "I'm glad that they've finally discovered each other. Speaking of which, I'm off to find my better half." He kissed her cheek.

Loneliness swept through Emily like the desert wind. Everyone seemed to have someone but her. "Nate, would you mind if I took Maggie out for a ride?"

"Make it a short one. There's a storm forecast for later."

Her brother's concern tugged at her already raw emotions. She gave him a quick hug. "Thanks for caring. Not just now, but all those years after Dad died, too. You've been the best brother a girl could have."

He frowned. "What brought that on?"

She shrugged. "I just never told you what a good job you've done."

He didn't look convinced. "Just so you know, you've turned out pretty good yourself. If I haven't said it before, I'm proud of you."

That did it. A tear found its way down her cheek. She brushed it away. "Oh, go find your wife." She gave him a shove and walked off toward the tack room. Picking up a saddle, she went to the mare's stall.

"Where you headed?"

She looked up. It was Camden. "Just a short ride."

"Is it okay if I tag along?" He looked as if he'd lost his best friend.

Maybe she didn't want to be alone, after all. "Sure, go saddle up Charlie."

Ten minutes later, they headed out of the corral. The late-afternoon temperature had cooled considerably. She glanced back just as Jenny came out of the bunkhouse. Emily waved, but the actress was too busy glaring at Camden to notice her.

The actor gave her a sideways glance. "You know, Emily, right now I want to forget everything and just ride."

Emily sighed. "I know the feeling."

"Then run away with me."

The past month of filming had been work but also a lot of fun. She'd learned to handle Camden's flirting, but at the same time she could sense his sadness.

"Is everything okay, Camden? I know Trent wasn't happy with today's work."

Camden adjusted his cowboy hat to shield his eyes from the sun. "Maybe some time away from the job might give me a new perspective." He raised an eyebrow. "Why don't you take me out to the old homestead?"

She wasn't crazy about the idea. "I'm not sure...."

"Come on, Emily, maybe I'll feel some connection I can use in the movie."

The homestead was farther than she'd planned to

go, and the terrain rougher, but if it would help the film... "Okay, but Trent will shoot me if anything happens to you so you're going to have to follow me and take my direction."

He gave her a slow sexy grin. "I'll do almost anything that will guarantee some time with you."

Thirty minutes later Emily and Camden rode though the grove of cottonwood trees to what was left of the original cabin Jacob Hunter built. The foundation, three of the walls and part of the roof had survived the past one hundred years.

Emily climbed down and tied her horse's reins to the old hitching post. Camden followed, and together they walked up the porch step and opened the door.

"Man, your brother did an incredible job of duplicating this cabin."

She preened with pride. "Shane is an excellent carpenter. I'll have to show you the custom homes he just finished in Paradise Estates."

Camden tested one of the rough-wood posts. "What's left of this has held up well." He walked over the threshold where the door hung cockeyed off its hinges. Most of the roof was gone, exposing the main living area, but the sleeping alcove was still protected by wood shingles.

"The barn out back has held up better," Emily explained. "Someday Nate is going to restore this cabin. But he wants to get the ranch up and running first."

"It's hard to believe that someone lived all the way out here."

She laughed. "Spoken like a true city-boy." A sudden breeze kicked up and she glanced at the threatening clouds moving in. "I think we should head back."

When she started to leave, Camden reached for her arm. "What's the hurry? We haven't had much of a chance to talk since filming began. That night at the Wild Mustang I barely got a dance."

Emily was confused. She was pretty certain this man had a thing for Jenny. "Look, Camden," she began as she took a step back. "If we ever get back to the Mustang then I promise to save you another dance. But right now, I'm more concerned about the approaching storm and us making it back."

He smiled and came closer. "Maybe we'll get stuck and have to spend the night here."

She held up her hand. "Okay, hold it right there. What about Jenny?"

He shrugged. "What about her?"

"Come on, Camden. I see the way you look at her and the way she looks back."

"That's over." He glanced away. "Her boyfriend is coming to visit her this weekend."

"I didn't know Jenny was seeing anyone."

He shook his head. "She says it's over, but the guy wants to try to work things out."

"Then why aren't you back there fighting for her. Unless you don't really care."

"She doesn't trust me."

"Well, you do have quite a reputation."

He glared. "You can't believe everything in the tabloids."

"Okay, I don't. But if you care about Jenny, make her believe it."

"How am I supposed to do that?"

"Go tell her how you feel. Maybe she wants you to fight for her."

"You think so?"

Before Emily could answer, a rider appeared on the trail. It was Reece on Toby.

Camden recognized him, too. "Looks like we have company. And he looks upset that you're out here with me."

"I doubt it," Emily said, more angry than flattered.

"Maybe I can prove you wrong." He grabbed for her.

"Camden—"

"He gave her a quick kiss on the lips, then raised her head and winked at her. "I couldn't resist. Now, I'm going after the woman I love." He walked out. With a salute to Reece, he climbed on his horse and took off.

Emily watched as Reece marched up the steps into the cabin. He was wearing his usual faded jeans and dark T-shirt, covered by a denim jacket. Damn, the man could be a model.

"What are you doing here?" she demanded.

"That's what I should be asking you," he said angrily. "Have you lost your mind coming out here with that guy?"

She stiffened as the wind picked up. "I'm a grown woman and I can spend time with whoever I want. Besides, I didn't invite you here."

"Well, I decided to come anyway. Looks like I scared your lover boy off."

"Not that it's any of your business, but he went to find Jenny. That's who he really cares about." Emily turned away, praying he would leave before she fell apart.

After a few seconds, she heard the sound of his boot against the wooden floor as he walked toward her. "Jenny?"

She wanted to scream. She ached from wanting this man, and he thought she had Camden on her mind.

He placed his hand on her shoulder. "I came here because I thought you needed…"

"A friend?"

His tender gaze locked with hers. He started to speak when the sky darkened, dust and leaves began to dance, then the rain started. Not with a sprinkle, but a sudden downpour.

"Damn." Reece grabbed her by the hand and pulled her under the remaining roof. "It's going to be a long, wet ride back."

"We can't go back in a storm like this. The trail turns into a river. Oh, no, I hope Camden made it back."

"Like I care," Reece hissed. "We need to get the horses out of this."

"There's more shelter in the barn. Come on," she said and ran out into the rain. She grabbed Maggie's reins and rushed toward the weathered structure about fifty yards away. The big door was gone, and inside there was a damp musky smell, but they would be protected from the storm.

"I'm not sure who inhabits this barn, but the horses should be okay here." She pulled off her hat and shook it, then used her shirtsleeve to wipe the dampness from her face, but her jeans were soaked, chilling her skin.

Still angry, Emily didn't want to look or speak to Reece. She was too vulnerable right now. She needed to get away from him, before she fell into his arms. But thanks to the weather, it looked like she was stuck with him for who knew how long.

She tied Maggie to a stall gate, flipped up the stirrup, undid the cinch and pulled the saddle off.

Suddenly Reece was there and took it from her. He easily lifted it to the stall railing. Then he went to Toby and removed his saddle next.

Reece stayed busy tending to the horses, but he knew he had to face Emily. Hell, he should have minded his own business. Then they might not be in this mess.

Damn, he didn't want to care about Emily Hunter. He had no business caring about her. But the more he tried to stay away from her, the more he wanted her.

He glanced toward the end of the barn to see Emily staring out at the downpour. He'd acted like a fool. But when he found out Emily had left with Camden, and realized the storm was coming, he had no choice but to go after her. Then he saw Peters kissing her....

As he walked to Emily, he took out his cell phone and punched in the ranch's number.

After three rings, Nate answered. "Double H."

"Nate. It's Reece."

"Did you find them?"

"Yeah, your ranch hand was right. They were at the old cabin. Camden took off before the rain started, but we're not sure he made it back. We're holed up in the old barn."

"I'll send Mike out to look for him. If he makes it across the ravine, he should be okay. But it's too risky for you and Emily to try to make it back now. It's supposed to rain most of the night, so you stay put."

"All night?" Reece repeated and saw Emily's shoulders stiffen.

"There's no choice. I've got my own problems here. Tori's in labor."

"Tori's in labor!"

Emily swung around and reached for the phone. "Nate, is she okay?" she asked.

Reece watched the excitement play over her face. He knew how much she wanted to be there with her family.

"Okay, just tell her I love her." She frowned. "Yeah, I'll get to meet little Jake tomorrow." She finally smiled. "I love you, too. Bye."

Emily handed the phone back to Reece and he suddenly felt like a heel. "I'm sorry, Emily. You're missing the baby's birth."

"It's not your fault," she admitted. "I'm the one who rode out here." She swiped at the moisture on her cheeks as the wind and rain intensified outside. "Tori has Nate and my mom with her. I just wish…"

"We will. Tomorrow morning. Maybe Tori won't even have the baby tonight."

She glared at him. "Bite your tongue. That would mean a fourteen hour labor."

His mouth twitched. "I guess that would be pretty rough."

Emily shook her head. "Isn't it like a man to think he understands the pain of childbirth."

He raised his hands in surrender. "I might not know the pain, but I've delivered a few foals in my time."

She rolled those big beautiful blue eyes. "That doesn't mean you know what you're talking about." She got a dreamy look. "But Tori has Nate. He's there for her."

Reece found himself wondering what it would be like to have Emily carrying his child. His chest began to ache so badly he had to look away. What was he thinking? She wanted her career, not a man with a four-year-old child. He wandered back toward the horses, dialed Betty Hunter's number and talked to the baby-sitter, then to Sophie. He assured her that he'd see her in the morning.

Reece checked the horses again, then went to his saddle to untie the bedroll and the saddlebags. He always kept snacks in his bag when he was on location. He reached inside and pulled out two bottles of water, a bunch of carrots, two apples for Toby and Shadow and four energy bars.

Just maybe he had a peace offering.

* * *

An hour after the sun had set, Emily grudgingly picked at Reece's makeshift meal. A small campfire in the doorway added dim light and helped ward off the chill. A blanket was spread out, with bottled water, apples and energy bars. If her stomach hadn't growled loudly, she'd have refused the food. But she was hungry and cold and tired. Seeing the small size of the blanket, she wasn't sure how they could make it through the night. The temperature had dropped twenty degrees and the rain hadn't let up at all.

Reece took another swig from the bottle of water, then replaced the cap. "That wasn't bad." When he didn't get any response from Emily, he took two of the carrots and went to feed the horses. After the animals were settled for the night, he came back to the fire and placed another piece of broken stall gate on the fire. "We're going to have to think about sleeping arrangements."

"You can sleep, I'm not tired."

"Considering that you're sitting on my the blanket that's going to be difficult."

"Excuse me." She stood and walked away.

"Stop it, Emily. I'm not the enemy here. I'm just trying to make the best of the situation."

"All of a sudden you want to talk to me." She glared at him. "For the past two weeks, if it wasn't for Sophie, you've barely given me the time of day. What did I do to you?"

He saw the tears in her eyes before she turned away.

His chest tightened. Man, it killed him to see her hurting. He stood. "Emily, I didn't mean to shut you out."

She swung around. "Well, you did, ever since the night in the apartment, when you kissed me. What happened, Reece? Did I get too close? Are you worried I'm going to want too much?"

He tried not to flinch when she hit his vulnerable spot. "I can't make you any promises, Emily," he whispered. "Besides, we're headed in different directions."

"Then why can't we be friends like you said?"

"Because I find it really difficult being just your friend." He raked his fingers through his hair. "I wish I could…"

She took a step closer. She was so beautiful it made him hurt.

"I don't need anything but you." She rose up and placed her mouth on his and suddenly all reason went out of the barn door as he reached out to take what was offered.

Chapter Nine

Never in my life had I been so afraid as when I
saw my Becky fall into the rain-swollen river. The
minutes seemed like an eternity until I reached her
and pulled her out. And I'd made every promise
I could think of to God so that he would keep her
and my child safe. He answered my prayers.
Jacob's Journal

Reece had never tasted anything as sweet, or as intoxicating, as Emily. Her kisses made him weak and strong
all at the same time. He drew her closer, and moved his
arms around her back, then down to her hips cradling
her body to his. He groaned. She felt so damn good.

He broke off the kiss and looked down at her shad-
owed face, seeing her incredible beauty. Her piercing

blue eyes. He'd never wanted anyone so much that it made him ache.

"Emily..." he breathed, dipping his head to meet her mouth in another earth-shattering kiss. He didn't want to think about how foolish this was. He already had too many complications in his life to even think they had a chance. But at the moment all he cared about was Emily.

Reece shook as he trailed his mouth down her slender neck, inflamed by her scent, her softness. When she moaned he lost any coherent thoughts, and he picked her up in his arms and carried her toward the fire.

He set her down on the blanket. "I hope you don't mind sharing the bed because you're going to have a hellvua time getting rid of me," he breathed against her ear.

She shivered. "Oh, Reece. Don't leave me." She lay back on the blanket, tugging at him to come with her.

"Sweetheart, I'm not going anywhere," he promised as he stretched out beside her. The firelight exposed the flush on her cheeks, the desire in her eyes. He kissed her again, this time tasting her hunger, her need as she melted into his arms.

Emily got a sudden rush of pleasure as Reece's hands worked the buttons on her blouse, then reached inside to touch her. She whimpered against his mouth, praying he wouldn't stop. She wanted him so much.

His breath caught as she turned the tables, opened his shirt and ran her fingers over his sculptured chest. "You have a beautiful body," she whispered.

"Oh, darlin'. You're the one who's beautiful." His heated gaze roamed up her long legs to her hips, her flat stomach, then came to her bra. He reached out and released the front clasp exposing her breasts. "Perfection." He leaned forward and drew the tip into his mouth, tasting, laving her with his tongue. She gasped and arched against him as pleasure danced through her.

He pulled her to him for another scorching kiss, loving the sensation of her breasts against his chest.

"Reece," she whispered as his hands played over her body. "Oh, Reece."

"I want you, Emily." He pressed against her as her hips moved instinctively. He kissed her again and lost all sense of reason. There was just this night and Emily... His excitement grew when he sat up and stripped off his shirt, and he was as breathless when he went to work on her jeans.

Just then Reece's cell phone rang. He wanted to ignore it, but couldn't. Casting a last glance at the near-naked Emily revealed by the firelight, he turned away and dug his phone out of his discarded shirt.

He flipped it open. "Hello?"

"Hey, Reece," Nate said.

"Nate." He watched as Emily quickly dressed.

"How is it going out there?" Nate asked. "Staying warm and dry?"

Definitely warm enough. "We're managing. Hey, I thought you'd be at the hospital."

"I am at the hospital and things moved faster than we

anticipated." Reece could hear the excitement in Nate's voice. "Could I talk to Auntie Em?"

He turned to Emily. She'd buttoned her blouse. "It's your brother, Nate. I think there's some news you'll want to hear."

When she took the phone, Reece got up and walked to the doorway to give her some privacy, and so he could clear his head. The cool rain felt good against his skin and his commonsense began to return. What the hell had possessed him?

Emily came to him. "Tori had the baby. Seven pounds and two ounces. Jacob Edward Hunter. He's named after our great-great-grandfather, and our father, Edward." There were tears in her eyes. "Dad would be so pleased." She slipped her arms about his waist as if it were the most natural thing in the world.

Reece wrapped his arms around her, knowing their special world had been invaded by reality, and that was a good thing. He had responsibilities to Sophie, and the movie. He couldn't think about starting up anything with Emily, no matter how much he desired her. "Another generation of Hunters. Congratulations."

Emily didn't want to think she imagined it, but she felt Reece pull away from her. "Reece, what is happening here?" she asked. "I mean I know the phone call came at the wrong time, but—"

He moved back. "No, it came at the right time. Before we made a mistake."

She felt as if he'd slapped her. "Well, you really know how to make a girl feel special."

"That's just it, Emily. You are special." He nodded toward their makeshift bed by the fire. "I was going to take you in a barn."

"It was good enough for my great-great-grandmother. Rebecca and Jacob lived here for months before the cabin was finished." She made him look at her. "It doesn't matter where you are, Reece. Not if you care about that person you are with." There was a long silence before Emily finally spoke. "Oh, my mistake. I thought the feelings were mutual here."

"Dammit, Emily." He paced away, then came back to her. "That's not the issue. I'm not the man you need in your life. Since I was old enough to fend for myself I've been on my own. I've survived. Although I'll never be able to forgive myself for not being there for my sister after our mother abandoned us. I found Carrie a few years back. She didn't want anything to do with me."

"She couldn't blame you."

He shrugged as he stared out into the rainy night. "I took too long," He barely got the words out. "She was already mixed up with a bad crowd. I wasn't persistent enough and let her go off with that jerk of a boyfriend."

With tears in her eyes, Emily came to him. She didn't know it was possible to love someone so much. "She had to know you tried."

"Maybe. All I can think about now is Sophie. She's my family."

"You don't have to do this on your own."

"I have to find my own footing, before I can ask

someone to share a life with me." He looked her in the eye. "You have a career. I want a different life for Sophie. She deserves it."

Emily started to protest, but realized he wasn't going to listen.

"We should get some sleep," he said.

Reece placed a few more boards on the fire, then walked off toward the far end of the barn. As much as Emily ached to go after him, she knew that he would only reject her. Again. How many times did she have to be told that he didn't want anything from her?

The problem was how was she going to stop loving him?

"He's beautiful, Tori," Emily said as she held her infant nephew in her arms. He'd grabbed hold of her finger with a surprisingly strong grip.

"I think so, too." Tori smiled. She looked tired, but happy. "And labor wasn't so bad. Nate was a little panicked driving me here, but once we made it to the hospital he was a great coach. And he was with me all through Jake's delivery."

There was utter joy on Tori's face. "I hear you had quite an adventure, too," she said. "Of course it couldn't be too rough spending all night with Reece."

Emily shrugged, trying to play it down. "We waited out the storm in the barn. It was the only place that was somewhat dry. Reece built a fire in the doorway and we dined on some energy bars and fruit."

"Sounds pretty cozy to me."

Emily remembered being curled up by the fire, wishing Reece would come to her. Instead she lay awake listening as Reece moved around the barn. Finally at daybreak Shane had arrived with some of the crew.

"Reece has made it clear that he doesn't want a relationship."

"Come on, Emily. I've seen the way the man looks at you. He practically drools."

"You're wrong." Emily handed Jake back to his mother. "And it's better this way, Tori. I mean, Reece has Sophie to worry about, and I'll have my career in L.A."

"Sophie needs a mother, and you can write anywhere." Tori glanced down at her son.

Just then Nate walked in. He went straight to his wife and new son, placing a tender kiss on Tori's mouth, and stroking Jake's head he turned to his sister.

"What do you think of your new nephew?"

Seeing the pride on her brother's face, Emily smiled. "He's pretty special all right."

"If you stuck around for a while, we might just let you baby-sit. But you're gonna have to get in line behind Mom."

"Well, Grandma should have first priority," Emily said. "But I'll be available until the movie is finished."

Nate's smile disappeared. "The movie! That's the reasons I'm glad I found you. Camden Peters was just brought into the emergency room. Seems he took a tumble off his horse this morning and hurt his shoulder."

"What was he doing on a horse?" Emily waved off

Nate before he could answer. "I've got to get back to the ranch."

Emily grabbed her purse and hurried out, her mind on the precious time they'd lose if Camden was in the hospital. What else could go wrong? She didn't want to think about the delays that could shut down the movie altogether.

"Miss Betty said I can hold baby Jake when he comes home from the hospital," Sophie said from the backseat.

Through the sheeting rain, Reece turned off the highway toward the Double H. His niece had been talking nonstop since he'd finally gotten home just hours ago. He hadn't slept in over thirty-six hours. Not since he and Emily ridden back from the homestead.

Reece closed his eyes for a moment, recalling the feel of Emily in his arms.... It had taken everything he had in him to push her away. But there couldn't be a future for them, no matter how much he'd come to care about her. He wasn't the man she needed. He had no idea how to be a family man. Even with Sophie he was just treading water. What if he couldn't settle down in one place?

Sophie brought him back to the present. "But I have to sit down and hold the baby *real* careful," she added.

"We'll see," he told her.

"But I've been practicing with my bear." She held up her raggedy friend. "I can't wait to see the baby."

He didn't need to get any more involved with the

Hunter family. It was going to be hard enough to leave as it was, especially for Sophie. Now, with Camden's accident their time here might be cut even shorter.

Earlier this morning while the rain had stopped for a while, Trent had asked Reece to go over a simple riding scene with Camden. Of course, the actor hadn't listened and ended up taking a bad spill. He'd bruised his shoulder and sprained his ankle. They'd spent the next two hours in the emergency room. Fortunately the movie's star was okay. Yet Reece couldn't help but feel partly responsible.

With the rain and the accident, filming had been shut down. He had a feeling that was why Jason had called the meeting.

"Unca Reece, do you need to practice?"

"Practice what?"

"Practice how to hold a baby. You can use my bear."

His heart tripped as he glanced in the rearview mirror and saw her big trusting eyes. "I think too many people holding the baby might not be a good idea. Maybe I should wait until he's a little older."

She reached for the piece of paper next to her. "Do you think Tori and Jake will like my picture?"

"Sure they will."

She studied the crayon drawing of the tiny baby. "Unca Reece. I wish I could live here forever."

His chest felt tight. *So did he.* "Sophie, you know we have to go back to California someday."

He watched the solemn child turn toward the window. How many places had she lived in her short life?

How many had he? Too many to count. He wanted nothing more than to put an end to his wandering. To have a home. His thoughts turned to this place and to Emily. The familiar longing caused him to ache deep inside.

He parked next to the barn, climbed out and hurried around the truck to get Sophie. He swung Sophie into his arms and they went into the barn. Just in time to see Emily. She had changed into fresh jeans and a pink blouse that added color to her cheeks.

Reece placed his niece on the ground. "Emily!" Sophie cheered and took off toward her.

He wanted to do the same. Last night had left him raw. Hurting Emily was the last thing he'd wanted to do, but in the long run it was for the best.

"Hi," he said. "How is Camden?"

"He's resting comfortably in his trailer with Jenny at his bedside. He's out of commission for at least a week, maybe two." She lowered her voice. "Thanks to you."

He blinked. "Me? What did I have to do with it?"

"You're the stuntman on the set. Camden wasn't supposed to do much riding."

"Listen, he took it upon himself to show off for Jenny."

He saw the frustration and obvious strain on her face. "I don't know if we can survive this."

"I'm sorry, Emily," he told her.

She didn't look like she believed him.

So what did he care? "Look, I've got to talk to Jason," he said. "Come on, Sophie."

"But I want to go with Emily to see the baby. I have a picture for Tori." Sophie held up her paper.

"I can take it to her." Emily smiled down at the child. "How would you like to help me bake a cake to welcome Tori and Jake home?"

Sophie's eyes rounded. "Can I, Unca Reece?"

He looked at Emily. "You sure? You didn't get much sleep last night." As hard as he tried, he couldn't help remembering the passionate woman he'd held in his arms the night before.

"I wouldn't have offered if I didn't feel up to it," she said to Reece. Then she turned and took the girl's hand. "It's miserable weather, Sophie. And bad weather makes for great baking."

Reece wished he could take away all the pain he saw on Emily's face.

"Can I please, Unca Reece?"

"Yeah, but you mind Emily." He leaned down and hugged the child, finding he couldn't get through a day without a sweet hug from his tiny charge.

Reece turned and hurried off toward the bunkhouse where he found Jason and Trent. They didn't look happy. "Reece, thanks for coming in," Jason said.

"I just heard Camden's going to be all right."

Jason shook his head. "Just so you know, no one blames you. Camden said you told him to take it easy. He admits he was showing off."

"It doesn't help the situation," Trent said. "We've got to delay shooting."

"Can't we shoot around him?" Reece asked.

"It's still going to cost us money." Jason said. "A lot of money."

Trent and Jason exchanged a frustrated look, then the director excused himself and left. Reece turned back to Jason.

"Okay, Jason, tell me what's really going on."

The sandy haired producer puffed out a breath. "One of our backers heard about Camden's accident and pulled out."

"So, get another one."

Jason's hazel eyes showed defeat. "Don't you think I've tried? I've been on the phone the last three hours. Money was pretty tight as it was. And now this," he said and began to pace. "What am I going to tell Emily? She has a lot of her own money tied up in this project, too."

"What if I find you the money?" Reece asked.

Jason blinked. "You can't tell me you have enough lying around to toss away on a movie."

"A great movie. I could invest a few dollars."

"I know how hard you have been saving to buy that ranch. I couldn't let you do it. And, besides, you've got little Sophie to worry about. I can't take your money."

"Dammit, Jason, there's got to be a way to get the funds we need. You could ask the Hunters."

Again Jason shook his head. "They've given us the ranch, and built the set. Man, I just can't do it."

Reece was pacing now. "Okay, let's talk to the crew. I can work for no pay until the movie is completed. I bet others will, too."

Jason still didn't look convinced. "You have no idea how much money it takes."

"Hell, Camden is making a fortune. Surely he'll be willing to help. And there are other people in this town who would hate to see us shut down. We can't give up." He started for the door, but before he could leave Jason called to him.

"Does Emily know how you feel about her?"

Was it that obvious? The tough part of it was that Reece couldn't even call Jason a liar. Somehow Emily Hunter had gotten into his heart. He just couldn't let her know.

Emily smiled in envy as Tori carried a sleeping Jake to the cradle in the den where a changing table and numerous baby supplies had been set up to keep the new mother from having to run upstairs.

"Is he going to sleep a long time?" Sophie asked. She'd been curious about everything, including the feeding and diaper changing, and especially interested in the difference between boys and girls.

"We can hope he'll sleep until he gets hungry again," Tori answered. "Little babies and children need a lot of rest and food to grow."

"Is that why I have to eat my vegetables?"

"Yes, that's why," Emily answered.

"When does Jake get to eat vegetables?"

"Sophie, stop with the questions."

Everyone turned around. Reece was standing in the doorway with Nate. "Unca Reece." Sophie motioned eagerly with her hand. "Come and see Jake."

Reece glanced at Tori and she waved him in. Emily watched the big man bend over the cradle. "He sure is a tiny thing."

"He's gonna grow," Sophie assured him. "Do you know that Jake drinks his milk right from his mommy? Just like puppies and kitties?"

Reece blushed and Emily bit back a smile. "Yep, I heard that's the way they do it."

"Your niece has a hundred more questions for you." Tori said, trying to hide a smile. "But we'll save you for now. Emily and Sophie are helping me fix dinner. You *are* staying for dinner, Reece." She insisted, then turned to her husband. "You both can stay in here, but do not pick up the baby. I want him to sleep." She kissed her husband and the girls left.

Nate Hunter went to the cradle and just stared down at his son. "Man, isn't he incredible?"

Reece couldn't disagree. He could see the love and pride on the other man's face. "He's a miracle, all right." Reece moved closer, intrigued by the new life. This child wasn't going to want for anything, especially love.

Nate motioned Reece into the living room. "Okay, now that you've met Jake, what's the other reason you wanted to see me?"

Reece hesitated, then began, "The rain is delaying the filming, and now with Camden's accident—" Reece paused, almost chickening out "—Jason should be telling you."

"I'm asking you, Reece."

"Okay. With Camden's fall one of the backers pulled out."

"Does Emily know?"

Reece shook his head. "I was hoping we could find a way to solve the problem before telling her."

"How much do you need?"

"That you'll have to ask Jason. But I know he doesn't want to take any more from you or your family."

"Then where are you going to get the money?"

"Actually I've talked with Jenny and Camden, and they're willing to take less money, but for that they want a piece of the movie."

Nate arched an eyebrow. "You went to them?"

He nodded. "And the crew. They all want a small part of this movie."

"The Hunters wouldn't mind owning a piece."

"You already do. Your contributions got the project started."

"It's not going to do any good if we can't come up with more money."

"We have an idea. I've been wondering if the citizens of Haven would be interested in investing in the movie."

Nate smiled. "The people of Haven have always been there when we needed help. Shane would be the one to talk to. His father-in-law, Kurt Easton, just happens to be on the city council. All we can do is ask."

"Oh, no, I couldn't," Reece said.

"Why not? I can't think of anyone better," Nate told

him. "Anyhow you'll find the folks around here pretty easy to talk to. There's not a nicer place to make a home and raise a family. Wouldn't hurt for you to think about Haven as a place to settle down. The land is pretty reasonable."

Reece didn't want to think about hanging around. He couldn't, not with Emily here. Even though Emily would be in L.A., this was still her home. And seeing her and not having her would be too much for him to bear.

Chapter Ten

In the midst of the worst flood in history, our daughter, Emily Rebecca made her arrival into the world. Now with a child, I worry if we can make a go of it. I suggested to Becky, she and the baby should go home to her parents. But when she and little Emily boarded the train, I couldn't bear it, and went after them. Somehow we'll make it…together.
Jacob's Journal

The following evening the curious citizens of Haven crowded the high school auditorium. Jason and Trent, along with Camden and Jenny, were all up on stage talking to Councilman Kurt Easton and Mayor Ben Pryor. The Hunter family sat in the front row.

Reece stood in the back of the room, watching as Emily greeted people she'd probably known her entire life. People that loved her and would do anything for the famous citizen who'd come back home to film the area's history.

What was not to love? She was beautiful. He knew firsthand how her blue eyes mesmerized, making a man lose all commonsense. How her body made him want to spend a lifetime discovering her passion. She was the type of woman who made a man to think about a lot of things and to forget about a whole bunch else.

The mayor hit the gavel on the table and everyone scrambled for a seat. "I calling this special town meeting to order," he began. "I want to thank everyone for coming tonight. I think you're going to enjoy yourselves. First on the agenda, I'd like to introduce two of our guests, Jason Michaels, the producer of *Hunter's Haven,* and the movie's director, Trent Justice. Not to delay any longer, I'm going to bring Jason to the podium and let him tell you why we're all here."

Jason stepped to the microphone to a round of applause. "Thank you, everyone, for coming out. I also want to thank everyone for so graciously letting our film crew invade your community these past weeks."

"Thank you for bringing us Camden Peters," a woman called from the audience.

"And Jennifer Tate," a man yelled as the crowd broke into laughter.

"Well, then, I'm glad they came along. We all feel strongly about this project. But we've run into some problems. To be honest, money problems." Mumbles and groans throughout the auditorium. Jason held up his hand to quiet the crowd.

"I think you all know that the weather, along with Camden's injury, has caused us some delays. But we believe in this project so much that all the actors have agreed to take a large reduction in their salaries, in exchange for a percentage of the movie's profits." Jason frowned. "We're still short, though. That's why we've come to you. We're offering to sell shares of *Hunter's Haven* to the citizens of Haven. Once the movie goes into theaters and makes a profit, you'll get dividends on your investment."

A hush fell over the crowd, but after a few seconds an older woman raised her hand and the mayor acknowledged her.

She made her way to the microphone. "I'm Emma Harris and I've known the Hunter family all my life." She smiled shyly as she turned to Nate. "I even had a crush on your grandfather." She looked at Emily. "And Emily, I think I speak for a lot of people when I say, we're so proud of you. And it's important that we preserve our history. So I would like to purchase the first share. But I do think to make this movie truly authentic, it would be nice if some of us townspeople could be in at least one of the scenes."

Now the crowd was buzzing.

Jason quieted them. "You want to be extras?"

"Sure," she said as the crowd cheered. "A lot of us ladies even have our own period costumes from when we celebrated frontier days."

Jason looked at Trent and the director nodded his approval. "Sure, why not," he said.

Reece pushed away from the wall and walked out the door. It looked like everything was going to work out. They could get the movie finished, and he and Sophie would be on their way. So, why didn't that make him feel good?

Even though it was raining again, and Camden's shoulder was still tender, they were back at work two days later. Emily was relieved that they had resolved all the problems for now, but she knew how close they'd come to the project being shut down. Thanks to the people of Haven, they'd sold enough shares to continue filming.

Today the crew set up the equipment under several large canopies along the narrow Rainbow River behind the cabin. She glanced at Reece who stood at the other end of a tarp, talking with Trent and Jenny about the upcoming scene. She'd avoided him as much as possible in hopes that not seeing him so much would quash her feelings for him, but no such luck. Many nights, she'd dreamed of the man, recalling how it felt to be in his arms, to taste his kisses. She quickly shook away her thoughts as the threesome walked toward her.

"Emily, talk some sense into Trent," Jenny began. "They're pulling Rebecca's flooded river scene. He says he's afraid I'll get hurt."

"We can't take that chance, Jen," Camden insisted, pulling her close, his protectiveness obvious.

Emily knew they couldn't afford another delay because of the weather. She glanced at the rain-swollen river, knowing surviving the wilderness was a central theme of the story. "How about if I do it?"

Trent stepped in "You're not a stunt woman, Emily."

"I know, but I grew up swimming in this river. Besides, it's only four feet deep. I'll sign a waiver, whatever you need. The movie needs this scene."

The director frowned, then finally looked at Reece. "You have a problem with her doing the scene?"

His face was impassive. "If she says she can handle it, she can handle it."

Thirty minutes later the rain was coming down even harder. Not as bad as the big flood of 1905, but the river looked threatening enough for this scene. They'd set up at the deepest part of the river and with the aid of some damming to raise the water level, it looked pretty realistic.

When Emily was dressed in period wardrobe—men's trousers, boots, a duster and a long blond wig—Reece put the horse's reins in her hands. "You are going after some stray calves on the other side of the river. When you get into the water about knee high, give Shadow her command to kneel. The water is about four feet deep, and when she goes down it'll look like she's lost her footing. Then slide off and push away." His gaze locked with her. "Just be careful, Emily."

She swallowed hard, surprised by his tenderness. "How long will I tread water until you come after me?"

"The current will pull you downstream some. I'm guessing about five minutes. But I'll be there."

"I know." Emily climbed up on Shadow, tugged her hat down, then wiped the heavy rain from her face. She rode to where Camden was on horseback tending the cattle, then Trent gave her the cue. Her heart raced as she kicked the horse's sides and Shadow took off for the rushing river.

At the water's edge, Emily headed toward the calves on the other side, and entered into the swift current. As instructed, Emily gave the command, and Shadow went down. She gasped as the cold water seeped into her clothes, weighing her down, making it difficult to maneuver.

She had a moment of panic as the current began to carry her. It was a lot stronger than she had expected and suddenly she struggled to find the bottom, but couldn't get traction. She went under, but quickly came up sputtering as she fought to keep afloat. Then Reece's strong arm circled her waist, pulling her up above the water.

"I've got you, darlin'," he told her, then his voice softened. "I'd never let anything happen to you."

She managed to relax and let him do the work and get them to the other side. Then he lifted her in his arms, carried her to the rocky shore and laid her down. Exhausted, he fell down nearly on top of her. Emily reveled in the feel of his body cradled with hers. When he raised his head and looked at her, she saw the flash of desire in his eyes.

"Are you okay?" he breathed raggedly.

She managed to nod. "A little frightened."

"Hell, you nearly scared me out of twenty years." His expression grew tender as he reached out to touch her face. "I don't know what I would have done if you…"

"Oh, Reece—" she gasped for air "—I'm okay, thanks to you."

"And cut!" Trent yelled.

Reece climbed to his feet, then helped her up. "You'd better get out of those wet clothes." He walked off to check on the horses, leaving Emily alone and miserable.

"Good job, Emily," Trent called from the other side of the river.

Jenny came to her side, holding a large umbrella over them. "That was one heck of a scene," she said. "Reece carrying you to shore was a nice touch."

Emily shook as one of the crew draped a blanket over her shoulders. She wasn't going to tell anyone how close to being swept away she really had been. "That was Trent's direction."

The blonde looked sheepish. "Funny, he didn't seem to know about it, but he's going to leave it in." She smiled. "You two are good together."

Emily glanced at Reece who was already across the river tending to the horses. As if he sensed her watching him, he turned in her direction. A shiver ran through her as she recalled how secure his touch had been when he held her.

"He's a good guy, Emily."

She turned back to Jenny. "I know. I just don't think he knows it."

The actress smiled. "Then I guess we're going to have to think of a way to convince him that you two belong together."

Emily shook her head. "Reece has made it clear that he doesn't want me in his life."

"I can't tell you how Camden had fought his feelings." She waved her hand. "You two just need a little help." The director called for Jenny and she started off, then turned around. "At the party tonight."

Emily remembered the celebration with the townspeople who helped support the movie. "I wasn't planning to go."

"Well, plan to."

Before Emily could protest, Jenny ran off. Her only consolation was that Reece wasn't likely to show up. For that she was grateful. A girl could take only so much rejection.

"You sure you have everything?" Reece asked his niece as she carried her backpack out of the apartment. They were both going to the party at the ranch, and Sophie was going to spend the night at Nate and Tori's. Reece had agreed only because he and Sophie didn't have much time left in Haven. So he'd relented tonight and let Sophie spend time with the Hunters and little Jake.

And he could check on Emily. He knew how quickly things could have turned bad today. When he'd seen her pulled under, he'd never been so scared in his life. He'd could have lost her. A tightening in chest had him sucking in a breath, realizing that he loved her.

Sophie broke into his reverie. "Yes, I got my 'jamas, toothbrush, my clothes for tomorrow and two dollies."

"What about Bear?"

The four-year-old rolled her big brown eyes. "Unca Reece, I'm not a baby anymore."

He fought a smile as he walked down the steps. "I guess I haven't been paying attention to how much you've grown up since we've been here."

"That's 'cause I like it here. I like my new friends." She stopped on the bottom step. "Why can't we stay here?"

Reece crouched down to her level. "Sophie, we've talked about this." This wasn't the time to hash it out again. "When the movie is finished we have to go back to California because that's where we live."

Her lower lip started to tremble. "But I don't have any friends there. I don't want to leave Emily and Tori…"

He didn't, either. "Remember, I told you about some-day going back to Texas and buying a place there."

"But I want to live here," she said stubbornly.

He couldn't do this now. "Hey, I think we better get to the party." He stood, walked his niece to the truck and strapped her inside. He went around to the other side, climbed in and started the engine.

"I got an idea, Unca Reece," she called from the back seat.

"What's that, sweetie?"

"You could marry Emily, then we can live here for-ever?"

* * *

Around ten o'clock the party started to wind down, and Emily wanted to retreat to the house before Jenny came up with any matchmaking ideas. Luckily Jenny's fans had kept her too occupied to think about Emily.

Emily made her escape, and hurried through the barn. As she passed by the stalls she couldn't help but stop and give attention to the occupants. Shadow in particular. They'd bonded in the past few days, especially after the river scene.

"How you doin', girl? A little lonely tonight?"

The mare whinnied and bobbed her head.

"I know the feeling. Too many people around for my taste. Mind if I keep you company for a while?"

"You're going to have to share," a familiar voice said.

Emily turned and saw him. Reece was coming toward her. He was dressed up for the party in new jeans and starched blue Western shirt.

"What are you doing here?"

"Pretty much the same thing you're doing. Getting away from the party, and checking on the horses."

She should leave. The last thing she wanted Reece to think was she was chasing after him.

"Well, I'll get out of your way.

He shrugged. "It's your barn, you have a right to be here if you want."

She stared at him, realizing that they were both uncomfortable. She flashed back to when he held her after he'd pulled her out of the river. She could have sworn that he cared for her. "It's better if I leave..."

Reece reached out and stopped her. "We don't always do what's best."

"Please, Reece, don't do this."

"I wish I could stop." He tugged her closer, then pauses before he lowered his mouth to hers.

There was nothing sweet about the kiss, only hunger and need. The most honest thing about Reece McKellen at the moment. Dazed, Emily whimpered as she wrapped her arms around his neck and returned that need. There was no denying her feelings for the man.

Reece broke off the kiss, breathing hard. "Damn, I can't seem to leave you alone."

"Then don't," she whispered.

"Emily, it wouldn't work between us."

"I don't think you've got a clue about what might work for *us*."

He studied her. "You want a career and Hollywood," he said. He pressed his forehead against hers and closed his eyes. "I can't ask you to give up your dream."

"What if I want—"

"No! I can't let you. I have nothing to offer you," he said.

How about your love? She cried silently.

"And I have Sophie to think about."

Her heart was breaking. How could he not know how much she loved that little girl.

"So when this movie is finished," he continued, "we're leaving and I'm taking Sophie to Texas."

She swallowed back the dryness in her throat. "So you're going to buy that ranch?"

"Eventually." He glanced away. "I just know that Hollywood isn't the place for Sophie or me, either."

She knew there was nothing more to be said. She felt the tears building, and fought them. "Well, I wish you and Sophie happiness. Good night, Reece." She held her head up and walked away.

By the time Emily reached the house, tears were welling in her eyes. She wanted to escape from the hurt but when she walked in the back door, she ran smack-dab into her mother in Sam's arms.

Betty jumped back. "Emily," she gasped. "You startled me."

"I'm sorry, Mom. Sam, I'll get out of your way in a second." She pointed to the back staircase. "I'm just going upstairs."

"Please, Emily, don't leave," her mother said. "Not until you tell us what's wrong."

Emily exhaled and smiled tentatively at Sam. "I'm just tired. And I don't want to put a damper on your evening." She hugged her mother. "I'm happy for you." She hugged Sam next. "I'm glad you have each other."

"How long have you known about us?" Sam stammered.

"Not long," she admitted. "I came by the house a few weeks ago and saw you kissing."

Betty sighed. "I guess we should have said something sooner."

Sam reached for Betty's hand. "What your mother is trying to say is, it took me long time to share my feelings with her. I want you to know that I'm not trying to take your father's place. It's just that I love your mother," he said.

Emily finally let the tears fall. "Oh, I'm so happy for you both. She hugged them again, at the same time she was fighting her own misery. "Now, I'm going to leave you alone. I need to check on Sophie and get some rest."

Emily rushed up the stairs and headed for her old bedroom as she brushed the tears off her cheeks. She sure hoped that Sophie was asleep because she couldn't handle any more drama tonight.

But when she opened the door and realized the bed was empty, she knew things were a lot worse.

Sophie was gone.

For the next hour, the entire family and the movie crew searched for one little four-year-old. They'd combed the house, as well as the barn and even the movie trailers.

"There are a lot of places around here that she could have gotten into," Nate told Reece. "As a kid, I had hundreds of hiding places. Do you know any reason why she would take off?"

Maybe because he was lousy at parenting, he told himself. "I know she wants to live here after the movie is finished. We talked about it again tonight," he said as Emily walked toward the group.

"I'm sorry, Reece," she said. "I should have checked on her."

"No, I shouldn't have come to the party. She's my responsibility."

Although Nate had retired as sheriff, he took charge of the search. "I'm going to talk to Cindy Cooper," he said. "She saw Sophie about sixty minutes ago headed toward the barn." He walked away leaving Emily and Reece alone.

Reece thought back to earlier when he and Emily were together in the barn. "She probably heard us talking."

"It's not your fault, Reece," she said.

"I couldn't make her feel secure enough." Flashes of his young sister came to mind. "It's just like Carrie. She needed me and I wasn't there for her, either."

Emily placed her hand on his arm. "Reece, you couldn't help that social services separated you two."

"Maybe I was relieved that we were sent to different places and I didn't have to worry about her anymore."

"You were a kid, Reece."

He raked his finger over his hair. "I should have been there when she needed me. She depended on me."

"Carrie knew you loved her. And she knew you'd be good to Sophie, or she'd never left her child for you to raise. And everyone can see how much you love Sophie." He saw the tears in Emily's eyes. "She's lucky to have you."

Reece felt his resolve crumble. "Oh, Emily, I can't lose her. If family services finds out she's run away they could take her from me."

"No, Reece, they won't. You're a great father." Her grip tightened. "And Sophie loves you."

"Thank you," he said as he drew her into his arms. He needed her strength, her confidence and her caring. He had feelings for her, too. Emily made him want things he'd only dreamed about. But she had her career, and he couldn't take that away. He finally took a step back and saw Shane and Mariah come toward them.

"Do you want some of the guys to look around on horseback?" Shane offered. "We can at least search a perimeter around the house."

Just then the soft sound of a kitten meowing drew their attention. The barn cat. "Where is Missy's litter?" Reece asked, recalling how fascinated Sophie had been about the new arrivals.

"She should be in the tack room," Emily said, looking puzzled. "But we've checked there."

Reece took off down the aisle, Emily right behind him. He opened the door to the dimly lit area, went directly to the saddles and the footlocker and found the small child curled up, one of the kittens in her arms.

"Sophie." Reece reached in and swung her into his arms. He hugged her tight, feeling every emotion surge to the surface and not caring. He loved this child. Unable to stand any longer, he sank down onto the small bunk, refusing to let her go. "Oh, sweetheart, I was so scared. Why did you run off?"

She shrugged. "I forgot to say good-night to the kitties. Then I saw you talking with Emily." The child looked at Emily. "You said we were going to leave soon. I don't want us to leave, Unca Reece."

"But running away isn't right, either," he told her. "You had everyone so worried."

"I'm sorry," Her lower lip trembled. "I promise I won't do it again." The tiny girl yawned and Emily took the kitten from her hand. "Why don't you talk some more in the morning. Right now it's time for bed."

While Nate called off the search, Emily walked along with Reece as he carried the sleeping child to the house. Once in the bedroom, Reece removed the child's slippers and tucked her under the covers.

He bent to kiss her, and she kissed him back. "I love you, Unca Reece."

His throat tightened. "I love you, too, sweetheart."

"I love you, too, Emily."

Emily kissed the girl. "I love you, too," she said and walked to the door.

Sophie called to her. "I wish I could live here forever and that you'd be my new mommy."

Reece watched the emotions play across Emily's face as she nodded, then left the room.

"Did I make Emily sad, Unca Reece?"

"No, I think everyone is just tired." He sank down to the edge of the bed. "Now, go to sleep."

The girl nodded, then a tear ran down her cheek. "I'm sorry, Unca Reece." She began to sob.

"Oh, sweetie, it's okay." He brushed back her hair. "We found you and that's all that matters."

"But Mommy said that I should listen to everything you say and be a good girl."

Reece was shocked. "Your mother talked about me."

The child nodded. "She'd tell me all the things you did when you were kids. She said you were the best brother ever."

Reece swallow the huge lump in his throat. Carrie had really thought that? "I didn't get to stay with your mom."

Sophie's tiny fingers wiped the tears from her face. "I know, but she said you played games and held her hand when she got scared. And you made up good stories."

"I loved your mother," he whispered. "She was the best thing in my life." He forced a smile as he touched her cheek. "Until you came along."

"And Mommy said that you will always take care of me. You know why?"

Unable to speak, Reece's shook his head.

"'Cause, you are the bestest unca in the whole wide world."

Reece stood on the back porch and tried to clear his mind of tonight's events. He wouldn't know what he'd do if he'd lost Sophie. During the past few months, she'd become so important to him and was now an inseparable part of his life.

The door opened and Nate stepped out. "How you doin'?"

"Counting my blessings."

Nate looked over the grounds. "I know what you mean. That little girl of yours has come to mean a lot to all of us."

"I'm sorry for all the trouble."

"That's what family and friends are for, to help out." Nate turned to him. "It's really hard for you to take people's help, isn't it?"

"I've always found it better not to depend on anyone."

"It surprises me how a man is so interested in helping everyone, can't allow anyone to return the favor."

"What do you mean?"

"You went to a lot of trouble to keep this movie afloat. Yet you worked hard so no one would know."

"Jason and Trent got the people to contribute the money. Besides, I didn't want Emily to think…"

"Emily's gotten to you, hasn't she?" Nate told him. "No use in denying it, I've seen a difference in her since the morning she came back from the homestead."

Reece's pulse sped up. "If you're worried, I can assure you, Nate, nothing happened."

"Whether it did or didn't, my sister is an adult and that's her business. My concern is that she may truly care for you and, if your obvious misery is any indication, I'd say you care about her."

"I'm not the man for her. My past and my future is so uncertain."

"We all have a past. You can't have much of a police record, or you'd never get custody of Sophie."

Reece shook his head. "Not since I was a juvenile. But I still can't offer Emily anything. I've got Sophie to think about."

Nate sighed and stretched his legs out in front of

him. "You know, I thought the same thing about Tori. I was crazy about her from the moment I laid eyes on her. Then I discovered she came from a well-to-do San Francisco family and I let her go back home because I didn't think she'd be happy living on a run-down ranch. Luckily I came to my senses and went after her."

There was a long silence. He tried not to think about the possibility of a life with Emily. "She wants to be in L.A. and have a career."

"And you want to raise horses. If you both do well enough, you can have a place in California and one here, too. I believe I mentioned to you that the Double H needs a ranch manager. If you have your heart set on your own place right away, there's a few sections of prime land that borders the Hunter property up for sale. I also know that it's available at a decent price."

Reece rubbed his hand over his face. He wanted to believe there was a place for him here, almost as much as he wanted to believe he and Emily could have a future together.

"Well, it looks like you've a lot to think about." Nate headed for the door, then paused. "Just so you know, when I didn't have enough money to buy this ranch back, the town came through and gave back a dozen of my figurines so I could have my first show. I was able to raise the money I needed from the proceeds of that show," he said. "So before you let your pride rule your heart, understand that everyone needs a helping hand sometimes."

"How do I know if Emily will even want a ready-made family?"

Nate cocked an eyebrow. "Sorry, fella, I can't help you there. You have to ask her that yourself."

Chapter Eleven

*The summer brings new promise. We've made it
through the worst and best of times here in the valley. The herd was sold and I bought a fine mare
to breed. Becky has planted sapling for her apple
orchard. All and all it's been a good year.*
Jacob's Journal

Emily slept fitfully during the night. Sharing a double
bed with a four-year-old wasn't very restful. And all she
could think about was how little time she had left with
Sophie. The movie was going to be completed soon, and
there would be no need for Reece to stay on.

When the sun rose she fought tears as she rolled
over and watched the little girl sleep. This was doubly
painful. Not only was she losing Reece, but she would
lose the child she'd come to love.

Sophie slowly opened her eyes. "Are you sad?"

Emily wiped away her tears and forced a smile. "No, just happy that we found you." She reached over and tickled the girl.

Sophie giggled. "I wasn't lost. I know everywhere to go on the ranch."

"You still have to be careful," Emily warned. "And never go anywhere unless your uncle knows about it."

The child nodded and brushed her tangled hair away from her cute heart-shaped face. "I know. They teached me at school. Don't talk to strangers. Scream and kick if a bad man tries to grab me. But Unca Reece won't let a bad man get me."

Emily smiled. "I know, but last night you scared him. He thought he'd lost you."

She bit her lip. "I told him I was sorry."

"I know, but maybe you should promise him that you'll never run away again."

"Will you go with me?"

Emily didn't want to be in the man's company any more than she had to be, but when Sophie asked, she didn't have the heart to turn her down. "Sure."

After they washed and got dressed, Sophie and Emily went down to the kitchen. Tori and Nate weren't around. Reece was at the stove, cooking breakfast.

He turned. "Good morning, ladies."

"Unca Reece," Sophie cried as she launched herself into his arms. "I promise I'll never, ever run away again."

"I'm glad." He gave the child a loud kiss on her cheek.

Seeing the handsome cowboy in his creased jeans and Western shirt made Emily want to be included in the lovefest. The apron tied around his waist did nothing to diminish his sex appeal, especially when he set his dark bedroom eyes on her. "Good morning, Emily."

"Morning, Reece. Where are Nate and Tori?" Please, don't leave me alone with this man.

"They went into town. It's Jake's first outing to the doctor." He smiled. "Looks like you're stuck with me."

"Are you cooking breakfast for us, Unca Reece?"

"I sure am." He set her down. "I'm making pancakes."

"Yeah." Sophie jumped up and down.

His attention turned back to her. "How about you? What would you like?"

Emily's chest tightened in longing. "I should get down to the bunkhouse and see about today's schedule." She started for the door.

Reece put a hand on her arm. "Trent and Jason went into town, to check out the town shot. They won't be back until later." He followed her to the door. "Please, have breakfast with us."

Oh, sure, she could just sit down and act as if she hadn't fallen head over heels in love, when all the man wanted was to be best buddies. She glanced at the sweet little girl and table set for three. A perfect family scene. Not right now. Not when her heart was breaking.

"I can't," she said softly and pulled open the door. She ran away from what she wanted more than anything else, and what she could never have.

* * *

Two hours later, Emily raced Maggie across the open range until she reached the cottonwood trees edging the old homestead. She tugged on the reins until the horse stopped, then climbed off and led her horse to get a drink from the water pump. Then Emily drank.

Even after the hard ride, she couldn't force Reece out of her head. The memories had finally drawn her here. Back to where they had shared a special time. She tied Maggie's reins to the tree and wandered toward the barn.

Inside there was little evidence left of their night together. Things they'd shared, and how closed they'd come. Somehow she had to find a way to stop thinking about him, to stop wanting him, to stop loving him.

She walked toward the remains of the fire where she and Reece had nearly made love. Her heart soared as she recalled the feeling of being in his arms. Tears pooled in her eyes and she angrily dashed them away.

Hearing a rider approach, she went to the doorway.

Her brother jumped off his gelding and marched toward her. "You know, it would be nice if you let someone know where you're going. You had us all worried."

Emily couldn't hold back any more and broke down. "I'm sorry. I needed to be by myself."

His expression softened. "Would this have anything to do with a certain stuntman?"

"I'm not going to talk about it."

Nate murmured something about being stubborn. He pulled out his cell phone and dialed a number as he walked away. He said something about her being found, then disconnected before turning back to her.

"You know, I didn't have this much trouble when I was trying to win Tori."

"That's because you and Tori loved each other." She wiped away the last of her tears. "I'm sorry. I'm just tired," she said and swallowed hard. What was wrong with her? She'd never been a crybaby? "I'll get over it."

"Do you want to?" he asked.

"I don't have a choice. The man doesn't want me."

Nate folded his arms. "Oh, yeah. That's the reason he's worked so hard to save the movie, by coming up with the idea to sell shares to the town. Reece also invested in *Hunter's Haven*. He gave up his salary for the project."

"He can't. He needs the money to buy his ranch."

Before Nate could say more another rider appeared. It was Reece. "Maybe he should explain himself," Nate told her. Reece jumped down from Toby and approached them. Nate nodded in greeting as he walked out, then mounted up and rode off.

She drank in the sight of Reece as he walked inside. The tall man with the brooding eyes, held secrets so deep she might never share them. And as much as he'd hurt her she couldn't stop loving him. She didn't know if she ever would. "Please, Reece. I don't want this right now. Why don't we chalk this all up as a good time. Whatever I'm feeling, I can deal with it."

Reece felt a little shaky as he came toward her. But he wasn't going to let that stop him. "I think we should talk."

She started to back up, but Reece reached for her and pulled her to him. Her resistance evaporated and she came willingly into his arms. He lowered his head until his lips touched her hair. "Emily," he breathed her name. "I don't want us to just be friends. I want it all." He tipped her head back and mouth captured her mouth in a searing kiss. Dear Lord, how could he have thought he could live without her? She made him hungry, made him want more than he ever dreamed. He realized he had to ease her fears. He finally pulled back, seeing the pain in her eyes. He was going to do everything to take it away.

"I guess I'm not doing a very good job of talking. But you're distracting as hell woman."

"It's okay, Reece," she soothed. "I know you can't offer me—"

"What I mean, Emily, is that I can't give you what you deserve, but I'm selfish enough not to want to give you up. I did it once, and I don't have the strength to do it again." He took her hand. "The night we spent here I wanted you so much. But with my disaster of a child-hood, I felt I couldn't be a good family man or a good husband." He swallowed hard. His heart was pounding so hard surely she could hear it. "Then Sophie came in-to my life and then you blew me away from the moment I walked into the café."

"You had the same effect on me."

"Good, because Sophie and I have become pretty fond of Arizona. I've decided to buy a ranch right here."

Even with her heart breaking, Emily tried to be brave. "Just where is this ranch?"

"It's the old Baker place," he told her. "The house needs some renovations, but the barn is sturdy. Thanks to Nate, Chuck Barker has agreed to sell to me. And until I can get my horse breeding business going, I'll be managing the Double H for Nate."

Her brother had a hand in this. How could he have. She tried a smile and almost made it. "That's great, Reece." She couldn't stand any more, and pulled away.

She tried to leave, but Reece's arm slipped around her waist from behind. His mouth against her ear, he whispered, "If you keep running, Emily, I'll just come after you."

She closed her eyes as a shiver ran through her. "Reece, why are you doing this?"

"Because I can't live without you." She tried to turn around to face him, but he stopped her. "Just hear me out, Emily. I don't know the right words to say. All I know is that if you leave me again, I don't know if I'll be able to survive it. I love you, Emily. I want us to make a life together." He paused and took a breath. "I know I've hurt you to the point that you might never forgive me. It was my own stupid pride that kept me from thinking we could have a future together. Please, tell me I have a chance and you won't throw my love back in my face."

Emily was shaking when Reece released her. She managed to turn around and see the pain in his eyes. "Say it again," she whispered.

A slight smile creased his mouth as he pulled her close. "I love you, Emily Hunter, with everything in me."

His words made her strong and weak at the same time. "Oh, Reece. I love you, too."

His mouth covered hers and by the time he released her, she could barely stand. "Damn. I guess I should have asked if you even wanted to live on a ranch. I mean, what about your career? Even though I'm retiring from stuntwork, I don't want you to give up your writing. If you want, we can live in both places. What do you think?"

She couldn't help but smile. "That depends on what kind of offer I get."

Reece gave her one of those rare grins of his. "I wish I were better at this." He surprised her and pulled off his hat, then dropped to one knee. "Emily Hunter, I love you with all my heart. I would be honored if you'd be my wife. And Sophie's mom."

Happy tears blurred her eyes. Not only would she get the man she loved, but the sweetest little girl. "Oh, Reece, yes, I'll marry you. And yes, I'll be Sophie's mom."

He stood and swung her up in his arms as he kissed her until they were both breathless. "Let's have a short engagement," he suggested. "I don't think I can keep my hands off you for long."

She smiled as he trailed kisses across her jaw toward her ear, causing warm shivers down her spine. She shut her eyes, enjoying the pleasure of his touch. "Think you can stand it until *Hunter's Haven* is finished?"

He groaned. "As long as I have you close by. And maybe we can sneak up here every so often."

Their solitude was interrupted when a SUV came

Epilogue

Our lives have truly been blessed once again with the birth of our son, Zachary Jacob. And we've suddenly outgrown our cabin. Although we're sorry to leave our first home, it's time. I found a nice spot to build a house that will hold a large, loving family. A place where generations of Hunters can live and discover what Becky and I found in this haven. The true meaning of family.
Jacob's Journal

Emily walked into the café and spotted Reece seated at the counter drinking a cup of coffee. Seeing her new husband, her heart started to race. Since their wedding a month ago, they'd only managed to be together about half that time.

She had been back and forth to L.A. working on the completion of *Hunter's Haven,* but now that was finished and she could finally come home to her family.

Home. To her that meant making a life with the man she'd married and the new daughter she'd come to love as much as if she'd given birth to her.

Emily glanced at her husband's reflection in the mirror behind the counter. He still hadn't seen her, giving her a chance to study his handsome face, those incredible eyes that conveyed his love for her over and over again.

That day in the barn when Reece had confessed his feelings for her, he'd also shared with her his memories of a rough childhood. Not to get sympathy, but to explain the demons he'd carried around for years. The way he showed his trust in her only made her love him more, and admire how hard he'd worked to make something of his life.

It also gave her an idea for her next story.

Suddenly the tiny, dark-haired Sophie walked through the kitchen doors. Emily had to smile on seeing the child dressed in a miniature version of the Good Time Café's standard waitress's uniform; a white fitted skirt and top with red piping along the collar and sleeves. On her feet she had white tennis shoes and her hair was tied up into a ponytail that swung back and forth as she walked to the booth across the room.

As if Sophie had done this several times before she carried menus to the customers and said, "Hi, welcome to the Good Time Café. I'm Sophie."

A group of women Emily recognized from the church all smiled and began fussing over the child. Emily was so engrossed in watching Sophie she didn't see Reece walk up to her.

He put his arms around her. "She's almost as cute in that uniform as you were, but you've got her in the leg department."

"So you noticed," she said as she turned in his arms.

"More than once," he said in a husky voice. His mouth closed over hers without regard to who was in the café. She didn't care, either, as she returned his kiss with an urgency of her own. It had been over a week since she'd been home.

He groaned. "I've missed you. I can't wait to get you home and…" His words drifted off as his mouth moved to her ear and whispered the rest of his promise. She shivered.

"Well, the movie is finished and I won't be going back to the coast for a while. So I'm going to hold you to it." She kissed him again.

He held her tighter. "I'm gonna do my best, darlin'."

She had no doubt. Reece had been a very attentive husband and he always kept his word.

When *Hunter's Haven* concluded on schedule, their small family wedding took place right on the movie set. In the cabin where Jacob and Rebecca had started their life together. After the ceremony and reception, they'd spent their honeymoon right there in the cabin. Tears filled Emily's eyes as she thought back to Reece's tender loving that night.

Emily pulled back. "I'm not going anywhere for a long time. I'm here to stay. As long as I have you and Sophie, I'm happy."

"Even if we're a little crowded."

Reality had hit the newlyweds when they returned from their honeymoon and had to deal with the routine of family life and a small child, in the close quarters of the two bedroom foreman's house. Their temporary home until Shane and Reece could do the renovations to the old Baker place. Although, Emily didn't care where she'd lived with her family as long as they were together.

She moved against Reece. "Oh, I don't know, I like being close to you."

He frowned at her. "Same here, but there isn't any space for you to work."

"When Sophie's in school, I'll do just fine writing at the kitchen table."

"Well, there's definitely room in our new house. I've talked with Shane and we thought the sunporch could be converted into an office for you."

Emily smiled, loving the idea of moving into the big old ranch house. Especially since her future office would overlook the corral. "I could probably get a lot of inspiration watching my cowboy work."

"If you keep looking at me like that, neither one of us is going to get any work done."

Before Emily could answer him, she heard a young voice call out, "Mommy! Mommy, you came home."

Emily turned to see Sophie running toward her. She knelt and caught the child as she rushed into her arms.

"Yes, I'm home, sweetie. This time for a long time."

She stood and admired Sophie. "Looks like you've kept busy."

"I got a job," Sophie said proudly. "Papa Sam is paying me a dollar an hour to work." She pulled some coins out of her apron pocket. "And people are giving me money because they say I do a good job."

"Wow, that's a lot of money." Emily glanced toward the kitchen as Sam walked out with her mother.

"Emily, you're back." Betty hugged her.

"So you finally made it home," Sam said.

"And just in time." Emily nodded toward the child. "I see you're still recruiting new waitresses."

"Yep, and Sophie here is one of the best I ever had," Sam told her. "You can't start training them too soon."

"Isn't she adorable?" Betty said, looking lovingly at her new grandchild.

As if on cue, Sophie twirled around. "I'm going to wear it to school on Friday for show-and-tell day."

Just then the door opened and Shane and Mariah entered. "So, this is where the family is," Shane said as he hugged his wife close. "We just came from the doctor."

"Oh, is everything okay?" Betty asked.

"It's fine," Mariah said, smiling.

"Sophie, it looks like you won't be the only girl in the family for long," Shane said. "We're having a baby girl, too."

Sophie jumped up and down. "Hooray, just what I wanted."

The door swung open again, admitting Nate, Tori and Jake.

"We're having a baby girl," Sophie cheered.

Nate looked at Emily and blinked. "You're—"

"—Not me. Mariah's having a girl," Emily said, feeling a blush warm her face. Reece's hold tightened, but she didn't dare look at him. If she did he'd see how much she wished it were true.

The family was busy congratulating Shane and Mariah when Reece whispered to her, "I wish it were us. I'd love nothing more than for you to be carrying our child. But that wouldn't be fair to you. Your career is important."

Emily pulled Reece behind the counter, away from the group. "And I can't think of anything I'd want more than making a baby with you. I love you so much. And besides, I can do both." She saw the tears in Reece's eyes. "I know it's crazy, but suddenly family seems to be the thing that's most important. Just let's wait until after the *Hunter's Haven's* premiere in April. Then I'm all yours."

He kissed her. "I love you, Emily McKellen."

Suddenly they looked around to see the Hunter family was watching them. "Don't let us stop you," Shane teased.

"They kiss all the time," Sophie added. "Sometimes they go into the bedroom and close the door."

Chuckles broke out. "I think we'll take this home," Reece said as he scooped up his daughter.

"Hold on a minute," Sam called out. He took Betty's

hand and drew her close. "We were the ones who called you all here. It's because we have an announcement." He swallowed. "I want you all to know that I love your mother very much, and I've asked her to marry me." He glanced at her with such love that the room grew silent. "She said yes."

The room broke out in cheers. Everyone exchanged hugs and loving wishes for the couple's happiness. It had taken Emily a while to realize what was the most important thing of all. Love.

She looked at her husband holding their daughter and her heart soared. Then he held out a hand to invite her into his embrace. She went eagerly and slipped her arm around Reece's waist.

Sophie hugged both her parents. "Mommy, Daddy. All my wishes came true."

Reece turned to Emily, and placed a tender kiss on her lips. "So have mine," he said. "So have mine."

* * * * *

SILHOUETTE *Romance*®

COMING NEXT MONTH

#1790 TAMING OF THE TWO—Elizabeth Harbison
Shakespeare in Love
Beyond old-fashioned, Kate Gregory's father is *ancient*-fashioned
and insists she find a man so that her younger sister can marry! Not
liking *that* ultimatum, Kate secretly enlists the help of her childhood
nemesis, Ben Devere. And it's not long before their pretend scenario
has Kate thinking that Father just might know best!

#1791 SNOWBOUND BABY—Susan Meier
Bryant Baby Bonanza
Desperate to deliver a check that would save his ranch, the last
place Cooper Bryant needed to be was stranded in a blizzard with
a beautiful stranger and her baby. As he gets to know his reluctant
housemate during cozy fireside chats, Cooper begins reassessing
his priorities. But once this interlude ends, will Cooper sacrifice
everything for the love that will save *him* from himself?

#1792 HIS SLEEPING BEAUTY—Carol Grace
Fairy-Tale Brides
Sarah Jennings leads a protected, isolated life. Until the night she
is caught sleepwalking in her relative's garden and rescued by her
handsome, cynical next-door neighbor. But as her midnight rescuer's
kisses awaken Sarah from her slumber, will Max Monroe's teachings
help her embrace life…and his love?

#1793 THE MARINE AND ME—Cathie Linz
When U.S. Marine Captain Steve Kozlowski learns that Chloe Johnson
is a far cry from the frumpy librarian he'd presumed her to be, he
feels betrayed by her previous presentation. But as the two pair up to
outwit her matchmaking grandmother, Steve's attraction to her has
him contemplating his most challenging tour of duty—matrimony!

SRCNM1005